Clara Christiana Morgan Chapin

Thumb Nail Sketches of White Ribbon Women

Clara Christiana Morgan Chapin

Thumb Nail Sketches of White Ribbon Women

ISBN/EAN: 9783337097455

Printed in Europe, USA, Canada, Australia, Japan

Cover: Foto ©Andreas Hilbeck / pixelio.de

More available books at **www.hansebooks.com**

THUMB NAIL SKETCHES

OF

WHITE RIBBON WOMEN.

OFFICIAL.

EDITED BY

CLARA C. CHAPIN

Editor of Books and Leaflets for the Woman's Temperance Publishing Association.

WOMAN'S TEMPERANCE PUBLISHING ASSOCIATION,
THE TEMPLE, CHICAGO.
1895.

INTRODUCTION.

To White-Ribboners Round the World:

THUMB NAIL SKETCHES will always be associated in the minds of W. C. T. U. women with the beloved name of Julia A. Ames, under whose able superintendency the first edition was issued in 1891, only a few weeks before her promotion to heavenly service. It is therefore with a feeling almost of intrusion that the present editor, even at the earnest request of those who knew Miss Ames best and loved her most, undertakes the task of bringing out this new and enlarged edition, giving to the book the more comprehensive character demanded by the increasing forces and widening influence of our organization.

Its purpose is not so much to emblazon the name and the fame of the persons herein "sketched"—though incidentally it cannot fail to do that—but rather to serve our workers everywhere by making them better acquainted with the personality of their leaders while those leaders still remain with us. We hope it may assist local unions in advertising speakers and perhaps induce Press superintendents to print from time to time some of these brief sketches of representative white-ribboners.

We regret that the book does not include biographies of more leaders in "other lands than ours," but our friends will understand that the limited time given for its compilation is the reason for the omission and that we hope to remedy this defect and perhaps many others in a later edition.

It may truly be said that the sins both of omission and of commission which may attach to the work are the result not of want of will, but rather, want of skill; that its faults must be ascribed not to the lack of earnest endeavor but rather to the lack of infallibility on the part of the editor and of those who by their contributions and their counsel have so kindly aided her in this undertaking. With the hope, therefore, that its faults will all be forgiven and forgotten we send the little book on its mission.

Yours in the tie that binds,

THE EDITOR.

Faneuil Hall.

Boston, Mass., U. S. A.

In this Historic Hall the first World's W. C. T. U. Convention was held in 1891.

INDEX.

COUNTRIES.

MARY CLEMENT LEAVITT.

World's

Woman's Christian Temperance Union.

Organized 1883.

GENERAL OFFICERS.

MARY CLEMENT LEAVITT.

Honorary President.

Mrs. Mary Clement Leavitt is of New England ancestry and culture. She conducted a private school in Boston for years, until her children were grown up. In 1883, having been President of the W. C. T. U. of Boston, and a National Organizer of the society, she accepted from Miss Willard, as President, a roving commission as a pioneer for the World's W. C. T. U., which was projected in that year. After a thorough canvass of the Pacific coast, Mrs. Leavitt sailed for the Sandwich Islands, going without money or price, the National W. C. T. U. being at that time unable to furnish financial help. Through the efforts of white-ribboners and Christian people in Honolulu, enough was collected to send Mrs. Leavitt on her way rejoicing to Australia. In 1884 the local unions raised $2,612 for Mrs. Leavitt, of which she declined to receive anything except in emergencies, $1,670 having been the amount forwarded to her by the National Treasurer. She worked in Australia for a year or two, then visited Japan, China, and India, going thence to Ceylon and Madagascar. In the last named island she was received handsomely by the Queen, who gave one hundred dollars to help her on her mission. Thence Mrs. Leavitt sailed for South Africa; thence to England, and after speaking in all its leading towns and cities visited Scandinavia, Germany, France, Italy, Greece, Egypt and the Holy Land. She also made a voyage up the Congo to see for herself the effects of the rum curse there, introduced by so-called Christian nations, and reported it in that interesting pamphlet, "The Liquor Traffic in Western Africa." During her entire trip she was entertained by Christian people and her expenses were on an average of but one thousand dollars a year.

This first mission of Mrs. Leavitt to foreign lands extended into forty-three different countries. In the eight years she traveled 100,000 miles, crossed the equator eight times, held over 1,600 meetings, involving the services of 229 different interpreters in forty-seven languages; formed 130 temperance societies (most of them W. C. T. Unions) and twenty-three branches of the White Cross movement. She returned to America for the Boston Convention and started upon her second trip in 1892 through South and Central America, Mexico and the Bermuda Islands. Mrs. Leavitt was for years Corresponding Secretary of the World's W. C. T. U. and chief correspondent of *The Union Signal* in foreign countries. She is the incarnation of self-respect, and of good-will toward all whom she meets and receives therefore universal respect and good-will wherever she goes.

FRANCES E. WILLARD.

President.

No woman of the age is more widely known or more generally beloved than Miss Frances E. Willard, founder and President of the World's Woman's Christian Temperance Union, and President of the National W. C. T. U. of the United States. All the world knows of her and of her works. She it is who more than any other has helped to bring about what she herself has designated the great discovery of the century, viz., the discovery of woman by woman. The great organization which belts the globe with its symbolic bands of white has been a mighty factor in the evolution of the "awakened woman," and that organization owes its power and prestige largely to the tireless brain, the loving heart, the clear and vigilant eye of Frances Willard.

Our Chieftain—as her American comrades love to call her—was born at Churchville, near Roches'er, New York, September 28, 1839, the daughter of Hon. Josiah F. and Mary Thompson Hill Willard, both of New England stock. Her girlhood was spent in Churchville, New York, Oberlin, Ohio, and Janesville, Wisconsin, whence the family removed to Evanston, Illinois, the Willard home through all succeeding years. Miss Willard is a graduate of the Northwestern University, and took the degree of A. M. from Syracuse University. She was for four years professor of Natural Science at the Northwestern Female College; one year preceptress of the Genesee Wesleyan Seminary, Lima, New York; two years traveled abroad, studying continental languages and the Fine Arts; in 1871 became President of the Woman's College and professor

FRANCES E. WILLARD.

of Æsthetics in the Northwestern University; in 1874 Corresponding Secretary of the National W. C. T. U.; 1877, was associated with Mr. Moody in evangelistic work in Boston; 1878 President of the W. C. T. U. of Illinois and editor of the Chicago *Daily Post;* and 1879 President of the National W. C. T. U.

In 1887, Miss Willard was elected President of the Woman's Council of the United States, formed from the confederated societies of women; in the same year she was elected to the General Conference of the Methodist Episcopal Church which represents one hundred annual conferences and two million church members, and in 1889 to the Æcumenical Conference of the same church by the Rock River Conference, but previous to said Council her name was thrown out by the Board of Control because she was a woman. She is the originator of the Great Petition against the alcohol and opium trade, which is to be presented to all governments, and which has already started on its tour around the world. She has been from the first one of the directors of the Woman's Temperance Publishing Association, and since the death of Miss Mary Allen West, editor-in-chief of *The Union Signal,* official organ of the World's and National W. C. T. U., also one of the board of directors of the National Temperance Hospital and of the Temperance Temple. Upon her return to this country in 1894, after a prolonged absence in England, whither she went as the guest of Lady Henry Somerset for rest and recuperation, the honorary degree of LL. D. was conferred upon her by the Ohio Wesleyan University, of which Dr. Bashford is president.

Besides the multifarious duties connected with the presidency of a World's and National organization, books, magazine articles, tracts, editorials, follow each other in quick succession from this busy brain. Even during the year and a half of enforced "rest," the Chieftain's vitalizing touch continued to be felt in every department of W. C. T. U. work; and now every hour is crowded with action or with thought that crystallizes into action — and all for humanity, for Miss Willard long ago learned that service to man is service to God. She is pre-eminently the *people's* friend, the friend of the oppressed, the struggling, the sorrowful. As one who knows her well, said, recently, "The surest way to Miss Willard's heart is to have a ' grievance.' "

She is sometimes called "America's uncrowned queen." Queen she is if reigning in the hearts of her countrywomen make her such. Uncrowned she is not; the insignia of royalty which rests upon her brow, though invisible to mortal eye, is such as a monarch might well envy.

LADY HENRY SOMERSET.

Vice-President.

Isabel, Lady Henry Somerset, was born in 1851. She is the eldest daughter of Earl and Countess Somers of Eastnor Castle, Ledbury, in Herefordshire England. Three miles from the grand old market town of Ledbury is Eastnor Castle, beautiful for situation, majestic in character and historic in surroundings. In sight, is the Herefordshire Beacons, the highest point on the Malvern Range, one of the strongest hill fortresses in Britain. For ages the same summit of this hill has been used for beacon-fires, whose heats have charred its ranges. At the approach of the Spanish Armada,

> Twelve counties saw the blaze
> On Malvern's lonely heignts,

and Eastnor Castle is the home of one who to-day stands as a beacon-light, not only for England, but for the world.

Having no brothers, Lady Henry Somerset succeeded to the inheritance of the vast estate of her father. The family has been long owners in County Kent, certainly as far back as the thirteenth century, and it numbers many illustrious men and women.

Born thus to an inheritance of culture, refinement and wealth, married in 1872 to Lord Somerset, second son of the Duke of Beaufort, receiving the crown of motherhood in 1874 by the birth of her only child, Lady Henry Somerset seemed to have all that the world can give. Her life was passed in the gayest of England's most aristocratic society, and with it she seemed content until 1885. What heavenly breezes swept her soul then we do not know, but the result is manifest. Amid all of life's gayety, she had felt deep spiritual longings, and now these spoke to her soul imperatively ; she listened to this heavenly voice, turned her back upon London and its gayeties and went to Eastnor Castle, there to spend several months with her Bible and God. She came forth from this interval of solitude the daughter of a King. The duty lying nearest her was the welfare of a large tenantry. At the very threshold of her care for these people she was confronted with the drink problem. This made her a temperance woman and worker. In 1885, in the little village of Ledbury, at her castle gates, she signed the pledge with forty of her tenants. She had large possessions in the east of London as well as in the beautiful hills of Kent that we have described, her tenants in the city numbering nearly one hundred thousand. Over these she felt her heart stirring like that of a mother, and she who had been the light of the West End drawing-rooms now went to

ANNA A. GORDON.

MISS JESSIE ACKERMAN.

LADY HENRY SOMERSET.

the London missions to seek and save those that were lost. Lady Henry became one of the chief supporters of the great work undertaken by Rev. Hugh Price Hughes in St. James Hall. She went to him and offered to receive into her country home some of the destitute souls in the slums of Soho ; she gave fêtes to probably ten thousand poor people at a time ; so Eastnor Castle had new visitors.

Mrs. Hannah Whitall Smith seems to have been the connecting link between Lady Henry Somerset and the British Women's Temperance Association. Mrs. Smith went to Ledbury to give a series of Bible Readings. Here they met and communed concerning the things of the Kingdom and each discovered in the other a kindred spirit. When God led Lady Henry into this wide sphere, He touched her lips with a coal from off the altar of inspiration. There is something fresh and un-hackneyed about her expressions. She comes into the philanthropies from another sphere and has learned none of the accustomed phrases. She takes broad views of the situation, and does not shrink from bringing temperance into politics by laying the responsibility upon the voters. As editor of the *Woman's Signal,* as administrator, and as leader of the B. W. T. A., she is wielding an immense influence on the side of right and truth. Lady Henry stands to-day in the foreground of modern reform, a radical of radicals, an orator among orators, all her varied gifts of mind and personality set apart—"not to be ministered unto, but to minister." "Few women," says Miss Willard, "have wrought so much good in space so brief ; we are but at the beginning of the story, and if life and health are spared for twenty years it will be written that while the men of England had their Shaftesbury, its women had their Somerset."

Upon her first visit to this country in 1891, to attend the World's Convention in Boston, she made for herself an enduring place in the hearts of American white-ribboners, and each succeeding visit has intensified their love and admiration. They love her first of all for her own sake—for her sweet graciousness and her beautiful consecration to a holy cause—and they love her for her sisterly ministrations to their Chieftain at a most critical time. Indeed the names of Frances Willard and Lady Henry Somerset will ever be linked together in the thought of the World's Woman's Christian Temperance Union as its two great leaders.

The sketch of the late Secretary of the World's W. C. T. U., Mrs. Mary A. Woodbridge, and that of its lamented Treasurer, Mrs. Ella F. M. Williams, will be found among those of other promoted comrades, on page 98.

ANNA A. GORDON.

Assistant Secretary.

Miss Anna Adams Gordon was born and bred in Boston. She is a graduate of the Newton High School, was a student in Mount Holyoke College, and has been for eighteen years Miss Willard's private secretary and coadjutor. Miss Gordon comes of a parentage of the best New England and Middle States ancestry. She is the author of "Marching Songs" and the Song Book of the Y's, many selections of which were composed and written by herself; also of "Questions Answered," covering the juvenile work undertaken by the white-ribboners. She has also compiled the "White-Ribbon Birthday Book," written entertainments for juvenile societies and during her extended travels has spoken to the children in schools, Chautauquas and conventions. As World's Superintendent of Juvenile work, Miss Gordon called together the wonderful exhibition of the Temperance Pledge Cards of the children of all nations at the World's Fair in Chicago, 1893. The Willard Fountain of which she is projector was contributed by dimes from children all over the world to the World's Fair city and stands at the entrance to Willard Hall, The Temple.

It is safe to say that in the ranks of ripe young Christian womanhood, there is none to whose record the words *Semper fidelis* could more fittingly apply, none whose industry and talents have contributed more to the temperance reform

---

ROUND-THE-WORLD-MISSIONARIES.

MARY CLEMENT LEAVITT.

Mrs. Mary Clement Leavitt, our first Round-the-World Missionary is Honorary President of the World's W. C. T. U., and her sketch will be found on p. 1.

JESSIE A. ACKERMAN.

Miss Jessie Ackerman, of California, second Round-the-World Missionary, is of New England parentage, with the fearless, forceful qualities essential in a pioneer reformer. She is a member of the Baptist church and an accredited speaker in her denomination, having been urged by leaders to "be a minister and done with it," since she is so, in

DR. KATE C. BUSHNELL.

MISS ALICE R. PALMER.

MRS. ELIZABETH WHEELER ANDREW.

effect. But the temperance work has her whole great heart, and has carried her to Alaska on a trip of observation for our society, thence to the National W. C. T. U. Convention, New York (1888), where she was made World's Organizer and whence she went to the Hawaiian Islands, Australia, Japan, China, India (including Siam), and returned to Australia, having been forbidden by her physicians to remain longer in Asia. She suffered greatly from fever and ailments resulting therefrom, and feared she must give up her work ; was divinely healed and helped until she became stronger and more effective than ever. She built up the Australian W. C. T. U. on the foundations laid by Mrs. Leavitt, and was made President of the Federated Australasian provinces, returning in 1893 to America for the World's Convention in Chicago. Miss Ackerman is the fortunate possessor of a strong physique, but her arduous labors of the past few years have necessitated prolonged rest, and she is now in England, the guest of Lady Henry Somerset, with a view to regaining health and strength. She is a speaker of unusual power, having both wit and pathos at her command and takes high rank as a popular lecturer.

ELIZABETH WHEELER ANDREW.

Every white-ribboner knows and loves Mrs. Andrew, third Round-the-World Missionary (in point of exodus). She was a minister's daughter and wife and a successful teacher. Small of figure, graceful in movement, irradiate in smile, hers is a face and a form to remember and to bless. But rich is she, above all else, in the knowledge of her heavenly Father's benediction on the heroic and unmatched mission in the cause of purity and womanhood, which she and her beloved friend, Dr. Kate C. Bushnell, have accomplished in India and other Eastern countries. The story of their remarkable and successful service is better known in England than in their native land, for the official investigation of their reports, all of which have been confirmed, have necessitated their remaining on English soil much of the time since their social purity crusade, which occupied the years of 1890-'93. Their revelations of the social horrors of the British soldiery in India and the existence of the state regulation of vice contrary to orders from the mother country, have resulted in a complete reorganization of the army and a liberation of the degraded women. Mrs. Andrew and Dr. Bushnell have also conducted with signal ability a campaign against the opium traffic in which England is so deeply involved, with China and Africa, particularly.

When in the United States, Mrs. Audrew's home is in Evanston, Illinois. Hers is one of the many honored names long associated with the editorial staff of *The Union Signal* and the Woman's Temperance Publishing Association.

KATE C. BUSHNELL.

Dr. Kate C. Bushnell is so closely linked with Mrs. Andrew in bonds of service and affection that it is difficult to write of her alone. All that has been said of her friend's wonderful mission since 1890 may be said of hers, for they have worked together as one soul. And even before that date Dr. Bushnell, who is still a young woman, had accomplished a remarkable work for social purity in exploring and exposing the infamous dens of white slave women in the lumber-camp regions of Wisconsin and Michigan. Her preseutation of this awful iniquity was so modestly yet thrillingly done that the wicked trembled and fled, and the good rose up and took action. Legislative enactments, consequent upon this exposé, have greatly lessened the opportunity for the procuress' crimes. It was in 1886 that Miss Willard called Dr. Bushnell into the purity work ; at that time she founded the "Anchorage Mission," for women, in Chicago, which has been such a beacon for safety and reform ever since. Since then she has spoken on her searching theme throughout the United States and the world, returning last year to China, where she had lived for many years as a medical missionary. Dr. Bushnell's home is also in Evanston, Illinois.

ALICE R. PALMER.

The fifth Round-the-World Missionary of the W. C. T. U., Miss Alice R. Palmer, was born in Indiana in 1856. Her father was of New England stock and her mother Scotch-Irish on the one side and "Ole Virginny blue" on the other. She became a radical abolitionist as soon as she was able to know the meaning of the word. Her education was received at the State Normal school and after completing the course she taught in the public schools of the state. She began to be interested in W. C. T. U. work in 1884. Though at that time totally ignorant of the effects of drink she admired the dauntless courage of the women, and, impressed with the consciousness that God was their teacher, she, as she says, "joined the class and learned too." Miss Palmer became State Organizer, and in 1892 upon the nomination of Miss Willard was appointed by the General Officers to the work in South Africa. From that time until the present year, 1895, she was most happily engaged in founding and strengthening the local unions that are springing up all through that great new country, in which our heroic Mrs. Leavitt was the pioneer. She is now taking a needed and well-earned rest at her home in Franklin, Indiana.

SUPERINTENDENTS OF DEPARTMENTS.

FRANCES J. BARNES.

No name is more familiar to the young women who have donned the white ribbon the world over, than that of Mrs. Frances J. Barnes, General Secretary of the Young Woman's Branch.

Born in Skaneateles, a lovely village on the shores of a beautiful lake in the western part of New York state, she passed a very happy childhood in the shelter of a Christian home. She was married in 1871 to Mr. Willis A. Barnes, a young lawyer, and has since then lived in New York with the exception of four years spent in Chicago.

Mrs. Barnes' Quaker training had taught her the value of woman's voice and opinion and had prepared her, when the Crusade came, to step into the temperance ranks and "lend her influence" to that cause. Her first public work, however, commenced a few years later when she was living in Chicago. There she met Miss Willard and was associated with her in conducting gospel temperance meetings in lower Farwell Hall.

At the National Convention held in Baltimore in 1878 Mrs. Barnes was made a member of the committee on young woman's work. It was made a department of work at the convention of 1880 and Mrs. Barnes was appointed National Superintendent, which position she filled until the fall of 1891, when the Young Woman's Christian Temperance Union was made a Branch of the National W. C. T. U. with Mrs. Barnes as General Secretary. Under her supervision the work has spread with ever increasing ratio and wherever the General Secretary goes her tact and winning ways, as well as her attractive manner of presenting what seems to prejudiced minds a threadbare subject, gain many adherents to the cause she loves. This influence has been especially manifested at parlor meetings where an assemblage of young ladies can be gathered by invitation who would not attend a public temperance meeting, but

who come as a compliment to the hostess, and then remain to be introduced to the speaker and to confess the power of her persuasive words.

In 1890 Mrs. Barnes went as fraternal delegate from the National W.
C. T. U. to the British Women's Temperance Association whose convention met in London.   Here she presented Young Woman's work, and
Lady Henry Somerset, President of the Association, accepted the superintendency of this department.   She spent several months traveling
in Great Britain and on the continent, and in 1893 again went to England where she was the guest of Lady Henry Somerset at Reigate for
some weeks.

This year, 1895, she made a trip to the Mediterranean and the Orient
as chaperon to a party of five young ladies, and as is her wont sowed
temperance seed by the wayside in the many countries visited.

For sketch of Miss Anna A. Gordon, Superintendent of Juvenile
work, see page 6.

MARY H. HUNT.

The World's and National Department, of Scientific Temperance
Instruction, of which Mrs. Mary H. Hunt, of Boston, is superintendent,
aims to secure such legislation as shall make the study and teaching of
the laws of health, with special reference to the effects of narcotics on
the human body and mind, obligatory throughout the entire system of
public education.

Inspiration and prophecy have received a new illustration in the
creation and development of this department.   It has been well said
that "No hero rises to greatness in an emergency" any more than the
oak tree rises to height of trunk and toughness of fiber when some
national exigency requires battleships.   Descent from a long line of
devout ancestors distinguished as preachers and educators furnished
Mrs. Hunt that quality of heart and brain demanded in creating this
great department.   Like a hardly understood whisper in the ear came
to her in 1878 the thought, "Teach the children the scientific facts
about alcohol to-day and you save the nation from drunkenness to-
morrow."   She quickly saw that the public school system must be the
vehicle for this scientific temperance education, and that suitable text-
books must be prepared.   By the grace of God she has been instrumental
in writing the laws on this subject in all the States and Territories of the

FRANCES J. BARNES.

United States except three. She set the standard for the many series of graded text-books which have been issued to meet the demands of these laws, and since 1892 has published a magazine called the *School Physiology Journal*, which is devoted to showing the best methods of teaching this subject in different grades of schools ; and also to collecting for the busy teacher valuable quotations from great authorities on all controverted points.

While this work has been going on at home, foreign countries have taken note and the temperance teaching of the world is being modeled after the American plan, and the American text-books form the basis of that teaching throughout the world. Already from England, India and Russia the most urgent appeals are made to Mrs. Hunt to come over and help them. To the reverent soul this world-wide movement marks the conserving, conquering power of One "not willing that any should perish."

ELIZABETH W. GREENWOOD.

Miss Elizabeth W. Greenwood, Evangelistic Superintendent World's and National W. C. T. U., has from the Crusade, held a unique and influential position in our ranks. The daughter of a lawyer, living on Brooklyn Heights, the entrée to a very different life has always been open to her; but from fourteen years of age, when she consecrated herself to Christ, she has been consumed by a passion to embody her highest ideal of intellectual Christian womanhood.

After years spent in tireless study and her graduation with highest honors from one of our leading colleges, she entered the W. C. T. U. army rarely gifted and equipped. As President of a large Union, Superintendent of Scientific Temperance Instruction in her state ; National Superintendent of Juvenile work ; World's and National Superintendent of Evangelistic work, she has displayed most varied powers and great consecration.

As lecturer, preacher, evangelist, she has held immense audiences in most conservative churches, while jails, asylums, factories and halls have been equally familiar with her persuasive voice. As a teacher of the Word, and a speaker to children she is unequaled. For twenty years Miss Greenwood has preached during the summer to a large congregation, near her country home, ministering also in homes, and at the grave. Her presence is everywhere a spiritual uplift to our work. She is of Methodist antecedents but for some years has been attending upon the ministry of Dr. Richard Storrs, of Brooklyn.

HANNAH WHITALL SMITH.

The gospel temperance movement has no leader more trusty and tried than Hannah Whitall Smith, Superintendent of Bible Readings, a "Friend, indeed," by ancestry and membership. Her Bible Readings and books have a world-wide fame. Mrs. Smith was born in that good-will city of the Quakers, Philadelphia, on the 17th of February, 1832. Her father, John M. Whitall, was distinguished in the City of Brotherly Love as one of its best citizens, and her mother moved, a queen, in that most democratic of fellowships, the Society of Friends. Mrs. Smith was brought up strictly in the "principles and testimonies" of the Society of Friends. At nineteen years of age, she married Robert Pearsall Smith, also a Friend, though of Huguenot ancestry. Theirs was a home of wealth and happiness from the beginning. Several children were born to them. Her best known book, "The Christian's Secret of a Happy Life," has passed through not less than forty editions and has been translated into a dozen languages, including the Chinese. Other volumes of Bible lessons have been published by her and for years her Bible Readings have been a prominent feature of the publications of the Woman's Temperance Publishing Association.

In 1874, while engaged with her husband in the marvelous Brighton meetings, Mrs. Smith heard the story of the wonderful Woman's Crusade. As Mary B. Willard said in her sketch of Mrs. Smith, "She must be a prehistoric member of the society, for she wrote in the Crusade year: 'There came a strange and secret whisper to my spirit that told me I was to join myself to those women, and then and there I became a member of the W. C. T. U.'" Mrs. Smith's home illustrates the consecration of wealth and culture to the higher possibilities of Christian living, and has done so for a lifetime past. She is one of the chief friends and counselors of Lady Henry Somerset, in the British Women's Temperance Association. Her only living son, Logan Smith, is a student in Oxford University. Mary, the eldest daughter, is the wife of Frank Costelloe, a graduate of Oxford, and a rising barrister in London. Alys, the younger daughter, graduated from Bryn Mawr College with high standing and was recently married to the Hon. Bertrand Russell, grandson of Lord John Russell, one of the Premiers of England, and brother of Earl Russell.

Hannah Whitall Smith is an ideal hostess and many an American white-ribboner can testify to the genial hospitality dispensed in the beautiful English home of Mr. and Mrs. Smith.

MRS. MARY H. HUNT.

MRS. J. K. BARNEY.

"Thy gentleness hath made me great." Those words of the Psalmist have always seemed to us to belong in an especial degree to the Superintendent of Penal work for the World's W. C. T. U., and the National Prison Evangelist, Mrs. J. K. Barney, of Providence, Rhode Island.

It is rarely indeed that the world sees such a combination of dauntless force and gentle persuasiveness. A wee little woman, with a voice like a silver bell, a modest, almost shrinking air, a face lighted from within, and a smile that is heaven's own sunbeam, she is just the type that a conservative of conservatives would call "womanly"; just the one to whom a motherless child would turn for comfort or to whom a sin-sick, disgraced girl could sob out her bitter repentance.

She was for five years President of the Rhode Island W. C. T. U., and National Superintendent of Penal work; later she accepted the superintendency for the World's Union. In her capacity as Prison Evangelist, she has visited the majority of penal institutions in this country, and not only do hundreds of men and women bless God for her coming, as the beginning of a new life for them, but through her wise agitation, many necessary reforms have been brought about in prison government.

The appointment of police matrons, which has proved so vital as a reform measure in our cities, originated in Mrs. Barney's thought, and was by her pushed to a successful issue. She is a speaker of unusual ability; her Bible Readings in particular being marvelous in their depth of thought and clearness of teaching. She has just completed a most successful six months' work in England, and won for herself there the same warmth and tenderness of love which is given her here.

JOSEPHINE R. NICHOLS.

Mrs. Josephine Nichols, of Indiana, Superintendent of Fairs and Expositions is a Kentuckian by birth and training, an Episcopalian in church relationship and prominent in Foreign and Home Mission work in her church. As a school-girl she evinced marked literary ability and at a very early age contributed to more than one Southern magazine. She married young and for many years devoted herself to the cares of home and family.

When the Woman's Crusade began Mrs. Nichols entered into the movement with all the enthusiasm of her nature and ever since has been speaking and working for temperance and woman's suffrage in America and Europe. She was President of the State W. C. T. U. of Indiana, and for some years National Superintendent of the department of State and County Fairs. Temperance restaurants, temperance cafés, temperance bazaars, temperance news-stands, temperance drinks, temperance picture galleries, temperance banners and embellishments of all kinds are a special study with this expert as teacher. Her work for the W. C. T. U. at the New Orleans, Paris, and Columbian Expositions has added immensely to the prestige of our organization throughout the world, the white-ribbon exhibits having taken high rank upon each occasion—as prizes and medals testify.

Mrs. Nichols is one of the most popular W. C. T. U. orators in the field. A woman of refinement and culture, pleasing appearance, original in thought and graceful in delivery, she is received everywhere with marked approbation.

HANNAH J. BAILEY.

Mrs. Hannah J. Bailey, of Maine, Superintendent of the department of Peace and International Arbitration, is a woman whose philanthropic works are known far beyond the limits of the white-ribbon organization. She was born at Cornwall-on-Hudson in 1839, afterwards residing at Plattekill, New York, where she has erected a fine country seat on the site of her old homestead. She is the eldest of eleven children, reared in the strong, peaceful principles of the Society of Friends, in which denomination her father was a minister and of which she is a prominent member, holding responsible positions in the church. In 1868 she was married to Moses Bailey, a wealthy and highly honored Friend, whose death in 1882 left a great shadow upon her life.

Having been a school teacher for ten years prior to her marriage, Mrs. Bailey brought to her field of labor in the W. C. T. U. a power for systematic work, which, added to a natural thoughtfulness of detail, makes her a valuable leader, and her appointment to her present office in the World's Union in 1888 was a most fitting one. In its interest she is untiring, editing two papers, distributing literature, traveling and employing a secretary, all at her own expense. Mrs. Bailey is one of the directors of the Woman's Temperance Publishing Association, and has been from the first one of the main pillars of that organization, extending to it both moral and financial support. She is well known to the National Convention as its time-keeper, it being her duty to strike a

HANNAH WHITALL SMITH.

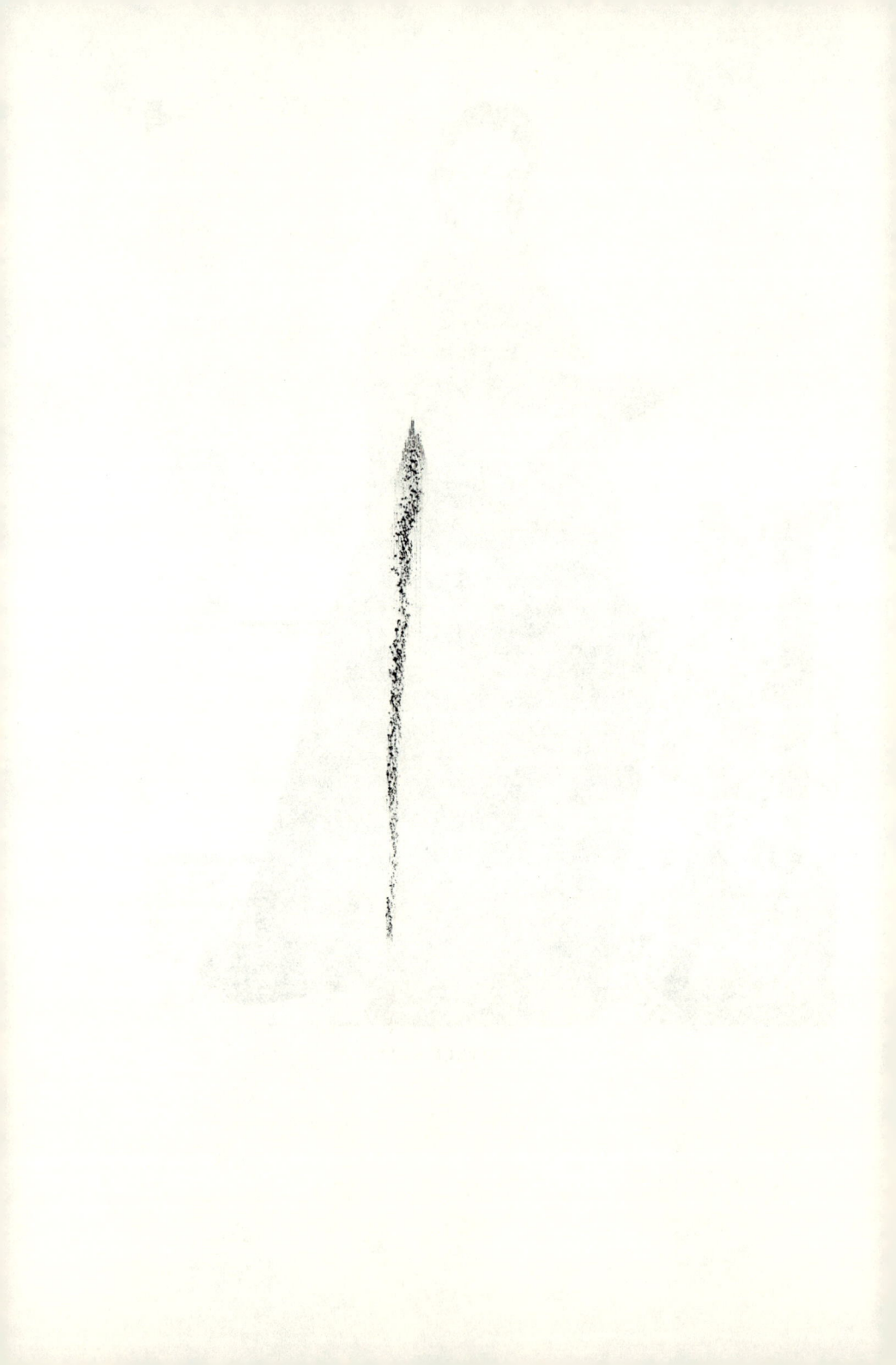

MRS. JOSEPHINE BUTLER.

bell on the instant that the allotment of any speaker expires. Her recent election as Treasurer of the National Council of Women shows a growing appreciation of her business ability.

Mrs. Bailey has one son, a Christian business man, who is worthy of his noble ancestry and his mother's greatest comfort.

LUCIA E. F. KIMBALL.

No department of W. C. T. U. effort can show a better record than that of Sunday-school work. Miss Lucia Kimball was its National Superintendent for seventeen years and has been three years World's Superintendent. She declares that whatever of good has been accomplished through her must be credited to her priceless heritage of Christian principles, and the example of her parents in loyalty to the temperance and all other noble causes. Miss Kimball was born and reared in New Hampshire, of parents noble in the truest sense, who in their childhood took a firm stand, amid much contradiction, for total abstinence. She is a graduate of Mt. Holyoke Seminary and was for several years a teacher in Chicago, but like many another, resigned her position that she might join the newly recruited army of the white-ribbon movement, and at once dedicated herself to work in the Sunday-schools. The largest Sunday-school petition ever known was the one circulated by her asking for a Quarterly Temperance Lesson in the International Series. This was acceded to at the Atlanta Sunday School Convention in 1878, but was subsequently thrown out by the International Committee.

Nothing daunted, Miss Kimball worked on until she succeeded in securing Quarterly Temperance Lessons in the regular course—a worldwide gain, as the International Series is used the world over.

Miss Kimball is an attractive writer and contributes to some of our leading religious weeklies, while her fine bearing, pleasant voice, clear enunciation and intense earnestness give her peculiar fitness as a public speaker.

MRS. CHARLTON EDHOLM.

Mrs. Charlton Edholm, who was appointed World's Superintendent of Press work, at the Boston Convention in 1891, has been a journalist for twenty years, most of her work being along Christian, temperance and philanthropic lines. For many years her work averaged two hundred and fifty columns of original matter, in which every phase of the labors of the W. C. T. U. was depicted in thousands of papers in the English-speaking world.

While editing that charming booklet, "Around the World with Jesus," by Evangelist Charles N. Crittenton, she became interested in the rescue work among erring girls, and her book entitled "The Traffic in Girls and Florence Crittenton Missions" was the result. Mrs. Edholm's heart became so stirred with love and pity for these betrayed and enslaved girls that she determined to make Social Purity work her specialty, and continues to both speak and write in their behalf. Wherever she speaks upon the subject and presents the splendid rescue work done by the thirteen Florence Crittenton Missions, her audience manifests intense interest, and an awakened desire to aid in saving the girls, and to that end many have joined the white-ribbon army. Mrs. Edholm's home is in Chicago where with her only son she leads a busy life in the work to which she has so fully consecrated her powers.

MRS. JOSEPHINE BUTLER.

No one can read the thrilling account of the Repeal Movement in England, of which Mrs. Josephine Butler was the heroic leader, without a sense of reverent love and thankfulness for such a brave and beautiful life. Mrs. Butler has worked for twenty-six years for the abolition of the state regulation of vice all over the world. She was married in 1850 to the Rev. George Butler, M. A., afterwards Canon of Winchester Cathedral, whose chivalrous love inspired her during the years of conflict before success crowned the efforts of the Repeal Party in 1886, when the Repeal Bill passed the House of Commons. What Mrs. Butler endured during the early stages of the campaign, few but herself know. Delicately nurtured and constitutionally sensitive, she had first to overcome a natural reluctance to speak out on the subject burning in her heart. The work began in Liverpool, where Mr. and Mrs. Butler opened a private House of Rest, and later, an Industrial Home for preventive and rescue work. "Then came," says Mrs. Butler, "the dreaded call to go forth and cry aloud," and though she "hated the task" the call was obeyed and the sacred fire of a new Crusade spread throughout Great Britain and the continent and has resulted in a wonderful awakening upon the subject of Social Purity the world over. Mrs. Butler's associates in this work for the World's W. C. T. U. are Mrs. Andrew and Dr. Bushnell, and a more consecrated and fearless trio it would be hard to find.

Mrs. Butler has filled the posts of President of Honor of the British Continental and General Federation for the abolition of state regulation of prostitution, and Continental Hon. Secretary of the same. Also, Hon. Secretary of the Ladies' National Association and is a member of the Executive Committee of the Personal Rights Association.

MISS AGNES WESTON.

Miss Weston, of Portsmouth, England, Superintendent of Work among Sailors for the World's W. C. T. U., is the President of the Plymouth Branch of the National B. W. T. A. For over twenty years she has lived and worked among the Blue Jackets of Her Majesty's Navy. The result of her powerful influence is now seen in the widespread reform which has taken place in the habits of hundreds of men to whom her name is a talisman for good. One man out of every six in the navy is a total abstainer, and Miss Weston's work—including her monthly letters to sailors—(the now far-famed "Blue-Backs"), *Ashore and Afloat*, which she edits, the "Sailors' Rests" she has established in Portsmouth, and her untiring personal efforts, have called forth the admiration, not only of the Commanders and the Lords of the Admiralty, but of all who know of the devoted labor of her life.

MISS CATHERINE GURNEY.

Miss Gurney, of London, World's Superintendent of Work among Policemen, is Hon. Secretary of the International Christian Police Association. The work which was started in her own home with six members, in 1893, has now become an International Association with branches in the United Kingdom, America, Australia, India, China, Japan and South Africa. The basis of the Association is entirely unsectarian and non-political, its object being the spiritual and temporal welfare of the police. It aims to establish Institutes, Convalescent Homes and Orphanages, and has a Police Temperance Union connected with it. For twenty-one years Miss Gurney has been a gospel temperance worker and for the last thirteen years connected with the work among the police, which she has now so successfully established in many lands.

MRS. S. L. OBERHOLTZER.

Mrs. S. L. Oberholtzer, of Norristown, Pennsylvania, poet and author, is Superintendent of School Savings Banks. She is an enthusiast in her line, as all specialists to be successful must be. This is comparatively a new department of W. C. T. U. work, but through the influence of Mrs. Oberholtzer there are hundreds of public schools in the United States following the Savings Banks system, proving that children thus trained to thought and economy by their teachers do not spend their money for cigarettes and drinks which breed intemperance.

As World's Superintendent of this most helpful department, Mrs. Oberholtzer hopes to introduce this system, which is proving so beneficial in our own country, into the W. C. T. U. work of other lands.

MRS. SHUTTLEWORTH BODEN.

Mrs. Boden, who is Superintendent of Parlor Meetings for the World's W. C. T .U. and Superintendent of the Social department of the National B. W. T. A., has been actively engaged in the white-ribbon cause for thirteen years. For some time she has interested herself in various ways in the women employés of Castle Fields Works (Messrs. Boden & Co.) and conducted a large sewing class weekly. She has had much to do with establishing and bringing to its present condition the Derby Branch of the National B. W. T. A.; has conducted and addressed many drawing-room and public meetings in various parts of the country and is greatly esteemed by all religious and philanthropic workers in the town, who regard her as their leader in many social and religious undertakings. She is the Vice-President of the British Temperance League, Vice-President of the Girls' Friendly Society, Treasurer of the Women's Union C. E. T. S. (Derby Branch), an active member of the Committee of the Association for the Help and Protection of Girls, and Vice-President of Derby and Derbyshire Bands of Hope, Woman's Auxiliary Union. Her husband, a wealthy manufacturer, has recently left the Conservative party on account of its opposition to the Local Veto Bill.

MISS GWENLLIAN MORGAN.

Miss Gwenllian Morgan, of Brecon, South Wales, Superintendent of Petitions and Treaties, World's W. C. T. U., is a member of the Executive Committee of the National B. W. T. A. and President of the Brecon

Branch. She has been a white-ribbon worker for eleven years and takes a deep interest in the work. Miss Morgan organized the Polyglot Petition work in Great Britain and Ireland and has filled the position of British Secretary for the World's W. C. T. U. Apart from this, she is in full sympathy with, and has long been connected with active work for women generally, on political and suffrage lines.

MRS. EVA MC LAREN.

The woman's movement in England has few more capable and popular supporters than Mrs. Eva McLaren, Superintendent of the Franchise department of the World's W. C. T. U. She is actively associated with the Woman's Liberal Federation, and is the Vice-President of the National B. W. T. A. In this capacity she presides over and leads the white-ribbon forces in England when the President, Lady Henry Somerset, is absent from the post. Mrs. McLaren is superintendent of the department for work among municipal women voters; is an authority on parliamentary drill and rules and procedure in debate ; has written leaflets on the subject of " The Duties of Women on Parish and District Councils," and has the cause of woman's franchise greatly at heart. Mrs. McLaren is also a fine speaker. Her husband, Walter McLaren, M. P., is a nephew of John Bright and one of the chief champions of woman's cause in the British Parliament.

MRS. ESTHER T. PRITCHARD.

Mrs. Esther Tuttle Pritchard, of Indiana, World's Superintendent of Proportionate and Systematic Giving, is the daughter of a minister of the Society of Friends and is herself a preacher in that church. She edited for some years *The Friends' Missionary Advocate* and was a teacher in the Chicago Training School for Missions. Her husband's removal from Chicago to the pastorate of the Friends church, Kokomo, Indiana, severed her connection with the school and left her free to push the special work of her department. Seventeen State Unions have now adopted the department, while outside the W. C. T. U. ten Woman's Missionary Boards have been influenced to create a similar agency. The World's department is as yet in its incipiency, but a movement so evidently providential must, under the enthusiastic and able superintendency of Mrs. Pritchard, continue to advance.

National and Colonial Auxiliaries.

United States.

Organized 1874.

GENERAL OFFICERS.

FRANCES. E. WILLARD.

President.

For sketch of our National President see page 2.

LILLIAN M. N. STEVENS.

Vice-President-at-Large.

Mrs. Lillian M. N. Stevens was born in Dover, Maine, in 1844. She spent her early womanhood as a teacher, and married at the age of twenty-one. Her husband sympathizes with her in her work, and her only child, Gertrude, now Mrs. Leavitt of Portland, Maine, is her mother's helper in much of her public work.

In the summer of 1874 when Miss Willard went to Old Orchard, Maine, to speak on temperance and to organize a W. C. T. U., Mrs. Stevens was there, assisted in the organization of the Maine Union and was chosen its Treasurer, which position she held for three years. She was then elected President, and has been unanimously re-elected to that position each succeeding year. For thirteen years she was Assistant Recording Secretary of the National W. C. T. U., for one year Recording Secretary, and at the Cleveland Convention in 1894, was, on nomination of Miss Willard, elected Vice-President-at-Large of the National Union.

Besides filling these offices and leading the women of Maine as President of the constantly growing State W. C. T. U., working and speaking untiringly for it, Mrs. Stevens has carried on a great amount of work connected with the charities of her native state, being officially connected with several homes for the dependent classes. She has for

MRS. L. M. N. STEVENS.

years been the Maine representative in the National Conference of Charities and Correction. In 1892 she was appointed one of the Lady Managers of the World's Columbian Exposition, and had entire charge of preparing Maine's exhibit of Charities and Correction (homes, hospitals, asylums, etc.) which appeared in the Anthropological Building at the Fair. For three years she was Treasurer of the National Council of Women of the United States, and upon voluntarily retiring from that position, was placed in the cabinet of the Council and given the portfolio of Moral Reform.

Mrs. Stevens has always been a woman suffragist. Even as a child she observed that the times were "out of joint" and felt that this was largely due to the fact that humanity is unequally developed in the two fractions which make up the integer. When in 1876 Miss Willard introduced into the white-ribbon ranks the unwelcome discussion of the ballot for woman as the most helpful method of temperance reform, and led the argument for four years in the great conventions, Mrs. Stevens was one of her staunchest and most helpful allies, and it was at this time that their friendship was cemented by that unbreakable bond forged in the furnace of contradiction.

No woman in our organization is more loyal to its fundamental principles; none possesses in greater degree the universal confidence of its friends, men and women, and the good-will of its opponents, than "Mrs. Stevens of Maine." The National W. C. T. U. congratulate themselves upon the fact that it is this level-headed, womanly woman who "stands for" their beloved Miss Willard during the latter's enforced absences and frequent withdrawals from public participation in W. C. T. U. affairs. With Mrs. Stevens as first-mate, the National Union, heavily freighted as it is with "hopes of future years," may "sail on" as in the past, with a "faith triumphant o'er its fears."

KATHARINE LENTE STEVENSON.

Corresponding Secretary.

"Showing mercy unto the third and fourth generation of them that love me," is a spontaneous reflection as one looks upon the inspired face of the little woman whom the world knows as Katharine Lente Stevenson. If Methodism would send her out as the finished product of the system, Methodist fathers and grandfathers would be at a premium, for an electric brain, pioneer progressiveness, intrepid courage and inexorable love stamp the word and work of this daughter of the church.

Katharine Lente Stevenson was born in Copake, Columbia County, New York, May 8, 1853. Her father was Marvin R. Lente; her mother Hannah Lonzada. In her mother a rare physical beauty and queenly dignity of bearing were blended with high mental and spiritual endowment and an intense love for all things true and beautiful. On the mother's side also may be found that trace of Jewish blood which Du Maurier says is so precious, when diluted, and so essential to the world's best achievement. In 1881 the daughter graduated from the School of Theology of Boston University, the only woman in her class, and pronounced by the dean "the best balanced mind in the school." The refusal of the General Conference of the M. E. Church to recognize women as preachers terminated her ministry as associate pastor of the Methodist church in Allston, Massachusetts, but she says the cherished dream of her life is to be in charge of a church—Methodist if it may be, Independent if it must be.

As the wife of Mr. James Stevenson, a merchant of Boston, Newton, Massachusetts, was her home until 1893, when she came to Chicago as editor of the department of Books and Leaflets for the Woman's Temperance Publishing Association, and contributing editor to the *Union Signal*. In November, 1894, the National W. C. T. U. showed its appreciation of her two years' brave service—1891-93—as Corresponding Secretary of the Massachusetts W. C. T. U. by electing her to the same office in the National organization. Now from her high corner in National Headquarters Mrs. Stevenson is thinking the highest, hoping the most and believing the best for every work and worker in the great cause. Her broad plans, swift intuitions and spirit of love that "thinketh no evil," will make her a realizer and harmonizer along all W. C. T. U. lines. But humanity is her field and every movement that guarantees the uplift of human life toward the Christ standard claims her active loyalty. Her logic is as keen as her intuition. Nelson Sizer, the great phrenologist, said of her, years ago, "that intellect of yours is like a detective, it shadows an error till it either trees or burrows it."

The crown of Mrs. Stevenson's life, however, is not her exceptional success as a platform speaker, a writer and an officer, but as a homemaker. She has poured out a large life on a husband worthy of her. No "own" children call her mother, but thousands of "own mothers" would die to win the worshipful love and fealty with which she is enriched by the three lovely step-daughters whom she has molded to her own sweet ways.

MRS. KATHARINE LENTE STEVENSON.

CLARA C. HOFFMAN.

CLARA C. HOFFMAN.

Recording Secretary.

Mrs. Clara C. Hoffman, of Kansas City, is one of the best lecturers among the brilliant coterie that the National W. C. T. U. has drawn together. When she speaks none can choose but listen, whether the subject is agreeable to him or not. To a clear brain, ready wit, great originality and a fluent command of language, she adds a heart on fire with her theme, and an ardent longing to save human souls from the slavery of drink. Nature has endowed her with a deep, mellow, alto voice, strong and clear, making every word distinctly audible in the largest building or in the open air. With wonderful adaptability she suits her discourse to the audience before her, and holds their attention, whether it be the educated or the mission people of a city, the pupils of a college or the rough denizens of some remote country village.

Mrs. Hoffman was born in New York state, but became identified with the white-ribbon movement in Kansas City, Missouri, giving up her position as principal of a school to enter its ranks.

Under her wise leadership Missouri speedily became one of the best organized of states, while her growing power and popularity as a leader have been evidenced by the fact that for the last five years of her state presidency there has not been one ballot cast against her. At the Chicago Convention in 1893 she was made Assistant Recording Secretary, and at Cleveland, 1894, chosen Recording Secretary to succeed Mrs. L. M. N. Stevens, who became Vice-President-at-Large.

She was the delegate of the National W. C. T. U. at the Woman's Council in Washington and no speaker was received with more marked favor. To her was given the honor of reading the Great Petition at its first presentation before a National ruler, in the interview with President Cleveland, Feb. 19, 1895. Mrs. Hoffman will be one of the most honored delegates at the London Convention and cannot fail to make for herself a place in the hearts of the sisterhood abroad as well as at home.

FRANCES ESTILL BEAUCHAMP.

Assistant Recording Secretary.

In a typical old Kentucky home where four generations of Estills had lived and died, Frances, the sole representative of the fifth Generation, was born in 1857. Of Quaker ancestry and reared under the

most happy Christian influences she early developed that sunny temperament and independence of thought which characterizes her. She was
given every educational advantage and graduated in 1874; was married
the following year to Mr. J. H. Beauchamp, a rising young lawyer and
Christian gentleman. When the Lexington W. C. T. U. was organized
in 1886, Mrs. Beauchamp became its Corresponding Secretary. She was
soon made President, then State Corresponding Secretary and from that
time on has held various offices in the State Union, proving herself in
every sense a leader. She was appointed Assistant Recording Secretary
of the National at the Cleveland Convention.

With great personal attractions Mrs. Beauchamp unites a self-reliant
nature and a pronounced aptitude for affairs, but as one who knows her
well says, "The one word which best characterizes her is loyalty ; loyalty
to her dear old father who first taught her a larger liberty for women, loyalty to her husband whose wise counsel is ever at her service, loyalty to
her home, her friends, her church, her Sunday-school, and loyalty to
the W. C. T. U."

HELEN M. BARKER.

Treasurer.

Mrs. Helen Morton Barker is a woman of marked individuality and
of pronounced ability along so many varying lines that her character
may well be called symmetrical. She is of good New England parentage and was born in northern New York. Her father was a physician
and scientist ; her mother a teacher, and both were radical temperance
reformers. Mrs. Barker's Academic course was taken at Gouverneur
Wesleyan Seminary, and, after her graduation, she was for several years
principal of one of the graded schools of Oswego. After her marriage
to Rev. M. Barker she entered earnestly into church work, and was for
eight years secretary of Foreign Mission work in western New York.
It was in this field that her remarkable ability for platform speaking
first made itself manifest. When the W. C. T. U. was born into its wonderful life Mrs. Barker heard in it the divine call and dedicated herself
to its upbuilding. She was unanimously elected first president of Alle-
gany County, New York, and devoted herself with such zeal to its
thorough organization that it was speedily known as the best organized
county throughout the state, and Mrs. Barker was made State Organizer.

MRS. HELEN M. BARKER.

For eight years she was President of Dakota W. C. T. U., and during that time organized hundreds of unions and visited nearly every town in that great territory. The Dakotas, North, and South, bear witness to-day to her splendid toil. She was Dakota's representative on the Board of Lady Managers for the Columbian Exposition, where her business ability so impressed itself upon her colleagues that she was called to Mrs. Palmer's office as assistant and remained there for two years.

At the Chicago Convention in 1893 she was made National Treasurer. Her financial showing at Cleveland proved the choice to have been an inspired one, and she was re-elected with enthusiasm.

As a speaker Mrs. Barker is logical and persuasive, with a keen wit and a graceful, gracious bearing. As an Executive officer her ability is of the highest and her judgment most profound, while as a woman, whether viewed in the relation of wife, mother, friend, or comrade, she is unvaryingly just and kind, with a broad outlook upon humanity's needs and a grasp of faith upon the Infinite which makes her mighty, through God, to meet those needs.

MINNIE B. HORNING.

Office Secretary.

Mrs. Minnie B. Horning is the only daughter of Helen M. Barker, and has inherited much of her mother's push and executive ability. A native of New York, she graduated from Elmira College in 1880, and was awarded the highest honors of her class. For one year she was preceptress of the Cuba, New York graded school. In 1882 she was married to Rev. Frank M. Horning, and as a minister's wife showed great ability as a manager of organized work. As State Superintendent of Demorest Contests, District President, and State Organizer in South Dakota, she became familiar with all lines of our work. At Headquarters she is lovingly spoken of as our Bureau of Information.

STATE PRESIDENTS.

Mrs. Martha L. Spencer has recently been elected for the fourth time by an enthusiastic and unanimous vote President of the Alabama W. C. T. U. The W. C. T. U. of Alabama knew what they were about when they rose as one woman to put Mrs. Spencer at the head of their band of devoted workers again. The organization has progressed steadily in weight of influence, increase of membership, in earnestness, and in spirituality under her administration. Mrs. Spencer was born in western New York. In 1881 she came South, adopting Alabama as her home, and bestowing on that state the inestimable gift of her life's best work in the cause of temperance. She entered the W. C. T. U. work in 1885, during the State Convention in Birmingham. In 1888 she was elected state corresponding secretary, and in 1891 State president. She is also president of the board of managers of the Mercy Home, under the auspices of the W. C. T. U. of Birmingham, an institution which is one of the most potent factors for good in that city. She comes by inheritance to her work as temperance reformer; her father, one of the pioneers of Orleans county having been for many years prominent in the old and influential order of the Sons of Temperance. Mrs. Spencer is the ideal presiding officer; firm, gentle, steady and progressive, her dignity and grace that of one of "ye courtly dames" of olden times. The smile with which she meets and well-nigh dissolves every difficulty of a convention discussion is the very incarnation of Southern sunshine. Her annual addresses are masterpieces of their kind, concise, clear-cut and elegant in style; in matter full, wide-reaching; above all, rich in spirituality and replete with the tenderness of loving kindness.

Mrs. John G. Brady of Sitka, is W. C. T. U. President of Alaska White-ribboners will regret that the sketch solicited by the editor did not reach us in time to be given here.

Mrs. Kate Hill Watrous, our leader in Arizona, was born in Pennsylvania in 1838. She began teaching at fourteen and continued to teach and study until her marriage, in 1859, to Mr. James Watrous, of Marshfield, Pennsylvania. A few years after they removed to Illinois, which state was their home for nearly twenty years. From there they removed to their present home in Tempe, Arizona. Mrs. Watrous has been a devoted Christian temperance worker from her youth up, and for six years has been closely connected with white-ribbon work.

Mrs. Fannie L. Chunn, the recently elected President of Arkansas, was born 1846; is descended on her mother's side from the old Kentucky family of Swans, and on the paternal side from the Hills of New York. Her birthplace, Cotton Plant, Woodruff County, Arkansas, is still her home. She was educated at Mary Sharp College, Winchester, Tennessee. An early marriage with its consequent home duties gave few leisure hours for the cultivation of a literary taste; but amid the varied demands of home and social life much reading was done, and an occasional article written for the press. Since 1886 Mrs. Chunn has been a zealous worker in the temperance cause and an ardent advocate of equal suffrage. She has been for the past four years recording and financial secretary of the Knights and Ladies of Honor and was a delegate to the Grand Lodge in May 1895. She is also corresponding secretary of the Equal Suffrage Association, of Arkansas.

Mrs. Sturtevant Peet, President of California, is a native of Vermont, and comes of an ancestry of that progressive quality which made New England's sons and daughters famous in history. When the great reform was inaugurated by the Crusade Mrs. Sturtevant was among the first to enlist. She served the Vermont W. C. T. U. as secretary and organizer for five years. Her husband, a brilliant young lawyer, having died in early manhood she afterwards married Mr. G. W. Peet of California, and at once became a leader of W. C. T. U. work in her adopted state. She was for six years President of Alameda county, and for four years has held the office of State President, a position for which her experience and natural tact admirably qualifies her. Mrs. Peet has been specially successful in legislative work and has spent three sessions in Sacramento in the interests of W. C. T. U. measures.

Mrs. Nancy P. Johnson Button, of South California, was born in Kirtland, Ohio of New England parents. When a child they came to Peoria county, Illinois, and there she grew to womanhood. She was under the efficient instruction of Mary Allen West in Galesburg, and later graduated from the State Normal Training School at Oswego, New

York. Always good disciplinarian, she was for some years a capable teacher in the graded schools of Aurora, and for five years principal of a large ward school in Bloomington, Illinois. In 1877 she married Rev. Charles Button, pastor of the Baptist church, Marquette, Michigan, and in 1880 moved with her husband to Riverside, California, their present home. Soon after the Crusade she became interested in the temperance cause and has since been actively engaged in the work. Mrs. Button was president of Southern California W. C. T. U. four consecutive years, and was again elected to that office in 1894.

Mary E. Cartland, President of North Carolina W. C. T. U., is the daughter of Jonathan and Elizabeth Cox, and a descendant through several generations of good old Quaker families of Virginia and Carolina. A liberal education has cultivated and enriched her fine native ability. Since her early childhood, all her powers of mind and soul have been consecrated to God, and her influence has been wide and beneficent. She was one of the first in the state to espouse the cause of the W. C. T. U., and has since that time been an important factor in all its undertakings. For several years as state superintendent of the Juvenile department, Mrs. Cartland labored unceasingly to gather the little ones under the protecting shield of the Triple Pledge. As president of the High Point union during a period of eight years, she performed valiant service for the cause of temperance in assisting to rid the town of saloons. She is faithful, energetic, prompt, always to be depended on to do the duty assigned her. Gentle and winning in her manner, immovable where principle is at stake, determined and courageous in the execution of plans of work, she is eminently fitted to lead her sisters in their peaceful war for God and Home and Humanity.

Mrs. M. J. O'Connell is President of the W. C. T. U. No. 2 (colored) of North Carolina. She is a graduate from college, and her husband, a man of rare eloquence, is pastor of the M. E. church in Greensboro. White-ribboners will regret with us that a fuller sketch of this faithful worker did not reach us in time to be published here.

Mrs. Sallie F. Chapin, who has been President of the South Carolina W. C. T. U. ever since its organization in 1880, was born, and reared in Charleston, the city in which her ancestors (who were Huguenots) came after the revocation of the "Edict of Nantes." She is highly educated, and a most brilliant conversationalist, and her home before the war was one of elegance and refinement. Her name has long been a household word in the South, known and loved through her writings, and in her own state, through her active leadership in patriotic, and philanthropic work. She was for years president of the Y. M. C. A. Auxiliary, and as president of a soldiers' relief society she did an untiring work during the war.

Mrs. Chapin joined the W. C. T. U. in 1880, and was immediately elected by the delegates from the fifteen Southern States, as Superintendent of Southern work. She has organized hundreds of unions, both white and colored, innumerable Bands of Hope, and in young men's colleges, some most successful White Cross societies. She is now experiencing the sad results of her heroic pioneer work, her health having entirely broken down. The last State Convention, however, refused even to consider her resignation and "Mrs. Chapin, sick or well, as long as she lives," was unanimously elected president for the fifteenth time. To Mrs. Chapin belongs the honor of first suggesting, and untiringly urging through legislature and press, the building of the Industrial School for girls, soon to be dedicated. The Scientific Temperance Bill passed through her efforts, and the pen with which the Governor signed it, and presented to Mrs. Chapin, was sent by her to Mrs. Hunt. To Mrs. Chapin more than to any other individual in the state, belongs the honor of bringing about the strong temperance sentiment which has closed all licensed barrooms, and which she thinks will result in prohibition.

Mrs. Eva C. Higgins, President of Colorado W. C. T. U., was born at Zanesville, Ohio, 1850, of Puritan parents. When she was thirteen years of age, the family moved to Michigan. She was educated at Albion College, and for five years before her marriage was a successful teacher. The last fourteen years have been spent in Colorado, where with improved health, Mrs. Higgins has worked in church and educational interests, as well as in the W. C. T. U. For two years she was principal of the public schools of La Veta, for eight years superintendent of a Sabbath-school, and at the same time president of the southern district W. C. T. U. She is a pleasing speaker and has done much for the cause of womanhood in Colorado, having traveled through valleys and over mountains, spreading the gospel of temperance and banding women together in the white-ribbon cause. Her husband and

daughter aid her in all good work.   Mrs. Higgins has been a member of
the Methodist church since fourteen years of age, and comes of a family
that has given many ministers and educators to this branch of the
church.

Mrs. Cornelia B. Forbes, of Hartford, Connecticut, is a typical
New England woman of excellent education and opportunities.   She
has held the office of President of the State W. C. T. U. for eleven
years.   Mrs. Forbes is the wife of a Congregational minister who was at
one time the Prohibition party's candidate for Governor.   To say this
is to make it apparent to those who read between the lines that this
devoted pair of temperance workers have the courage of their convictions.   They have borne the heat and burden of the day and rank
among the martyrs of the period, but they look exceedingly unlike
martyrs, being cheery, tranquil and as hard at work as ever.   Mrs.
Forbes made a strong impression on the National Convention at the
beginning, and in her character of Sergeant-at-arms, shows what a
womanly woman of vigorous physique, deep, strong voice and indomitable personality, can do in an unusual position which she neither
sought nor desired, but accepted as a soldier does sentry duty and a
picket-post.   Under her leadership Connecticut has done most excellent temperance work.

Miss Elizabeth Preston, President of North Dakota is a native
of the Hoosier State, and the only daughter of a Methodist minister,
Rev. E. S. Preston, who, for many years, did valiant service in this
state and in Minnesota.   She commenced teaching in her fifteenth
year and varied teaching with attending school until she entered the
temperance work six years ago, receiving her education at the Ft.
Wayne College, De Pauw University and the University of Minnesota
For four years she was State W. C. T. U. Organizer and Evangelist, and
in 1893 was elected standard bearer for the brave and loyal white-ribbon
army of North Dakota.   She has done most excellent work, giving all
her time and talent to the cause.   To her tact and untiring energy
through the last two legislatures the people of the state are largely
indebted for their prohibitory law.

Mrs. Emma A. Cranmer, President of South Dakota W. C. T. U.,
is one of our most successful workers.   The state union gained twenty-

five per cent in its membership last year under her leadership. Her native state is Wisconsin. The early years of her life were spent in Ohio, and when six years of age she came with her parents, to Iowa ; attended Cornell College, Iowa, for a number of years and was a successful teacher. She is the wife of Hon. S. H. Cranmer, an attorney of Aberdeen, where they reside. She is an ardent suffragist, having been at one time President of the South Dakota Equal Suffrage Association. Mrs. Cranmer is a member of the Methodist church, womanly in all her work and utterances and a strength to the cause of equality and temperance wherever she goes. She has written prose and poetry and is especially at home upon the platform, having lectured in various states with great success. She addressed the National W. C. T. U. Convention at Cleveland, and the National Council of Women at Washington.

Miss Margaret S. Hilles was elected President of Delaware in 1887, and was the youngest member of the National Executive Committee. Her father, a member of the Society of Friends and a man of wealth and culture, was one of the noblest Christian men who ever lived. In his daughter his own devoted spirit lives again, and the impulses which drew her into white-ribbon work were, to use her own expression, "a birthright." Her official relations to the organization have been local president, state superintendent of Young Woman's Work, superintendent of Scientific Temperance Instruction, recording secretary, and lastly state president. Her personal associations with our great leaders, especially with our beloved "Chieftain," have, Miss Hilles declares, proved a liberal education and a constant inspiration to her during all these years of labor in a cause which she "holds most sacred."

Mrs. Mary E. Griffith, President of the District of Columbia, is a native of Ohio and was among the leaders of the Crusade bands in the winter of 1873—74. She was married at nineteen to Mr. A. T. Griffith, a teacher by profession, and much of her life has been spent in college towns. She was state organizer of Juvenile work in Ohio, and removing to Illinois was for many years Superintendent of Evangelistic work in that state. During the Prohibitory Amendment campaign she gave five months' time to lecturing in Kansas. She was then elected general organizer of the Woman's Home Missionary Society, and spent five years traveling in the interests of that organization. Having removed

to Washington, District of Columbia, Mrs. Griffith was in 1893 made
president of the District. As a public speaker she takes high rank,
possesses marked power as a Bible teacher and is withal a woman of
superior executive ability.

Mrs. E. A. Hill, Florida's leader, is essentially a Western woman.
Though her birthplace was New York, she emigrated to Illinois in
early childhood, and from the broad free prairies of the West acquired
a wide range of vision—a broad outlook regarding men and things.
Her friends are accustomed to speak of her as "an all-around woman."
For twenty-five years a resident of the sunny South, she has devoted
time, means and talent to the upbuilding of temperance and other reforms. As state superintendent of Press work, as editor of the state
paper, and as president of the State W. C. T. U., she has served the
white-ribbon cause with a wisdom and faithfulness that has gained for
it and for herself an increasing power for good. It is safe to say that
the more tolerant spirit toward the reforms of the age, and the advanced
public sentiment which have become noticeable in Florida during the
past few years, are largely due to her efforts along the line of Christian
temperance.

Mrs. W. C. Sibley has been President of the Georgia W. C. T. U.
since Miss Willard founded it in 1881. She is the daughter of the distinguished Judge Thomas, of Columbus, Georgia, and wife of W. C. Sibley, President of Sibley Cotton Mills, one of the largest manufactories
in the South. From her elegant home where she is surrounded by
charming sons and daughters, she goes forth with her husband's hearty
indorsement, speaking (Presbyterian though she is) to her Christian
sisters, "that they go forward." Her first work for the W. C. T. U.
was done as president of the local union of the aristocratic old city of
Augusta. At the Atlanta Convention this sweet-natured lady stood
before a great audience, all unused to public speaking as she was, and
said: "Dear friends, I tell you truly if there were not another to stand
between the dram-shops of Georgia and its homes, so dearly do I love
this temperance cause, *I would stand there all alone.*"

Mrs. Georgia Swift King, President of Georgia Union No. 2
(colored), was born at Athens, Georgia, where she attended school for
Freedmen, taught by Northern teachers. She graduated from Atlanta

MRS. LOUISE S. ROUNDS.

University in 1874, and was principal of large schools at Athens and at Augusta, Georgia. She married in 1881 Mr. W. W. King, a bridge contractor, the union being blest with a son and daughter. In 1885 she was elected recording secretary of the first W. C. T. U. in the state of Georgia which admitted colored women as members.; afterwards president of the Fulton County W. C. T. U. During her three years as state president, Mrs. King has organized many local unions, and in speaking and lecturing has reached an average of five thousand people annually.

Mrs. Rebecca Mitchell, fourth President of the Idaho W. C. T. U., is an Illinois woman. Brought up by Christian parents she was early led to Christ, and was a member of the class of '82, of the Baptist Missionary Training School, Chicago. The needs of the great West stirred her heart, and without any knowledge as to her field of work, she reached Idaho Falls in June, 1882, working as a self-supporting missionary. She organized the first Baptist Sunday-school in eastern Idaho, the first Band of Hope in the territory and has since given her whole time to missionary and temperance work. She was first president of the local union in her town, and is now serving the State W. C. T. U. the fourth year as organizer and second year as president, with the double duties of superintendent of Evangelistic and Legislative work added. Mrs. Mitchell works on in a difficult field with unflinching self-sacrifice faith unwavering, sowing beside all waters with a zeal that knows no failure.

Mrs. Louise S. Rounds, of Illinois, is of New England parentage, being a lineal descendant of John Alden, of the *Mayflower* She spent some nine years in New York as a teacher, but has been a resident of Chicago for the last thirty years. She entered the temperance work with the first sound of the crusade bells, and has continued in it, bringing to the cause she loves the full force of her dauntless spirit and untiring energy. For several years she was secretary of the Central Union of that city, and had charge of its gospel meetings, which at one time numbered thirteen a week. Her husband died in New York in 1883. She was called back to Illinois by the State Executive Committee of the W. C. T. U., and was elected state evangelist, entering at once on her new duties. In 1886 she became state president, an office to which she has been annually re-elected since, by an enthusiastic following of loyal women, and in 1895 she was sent to represent her state in the World's W. C. T. U. Convention in London, England. As a speaker, she is earnest, logical and eloquent, and thoroughly uncompromising in her expression of hostility to the liquor traffic.

Mrs. Margaret Lena Adams Beck, President of the W. C. T. U. of Indiana, was born near Bloomington, Monroe County, Indiana, in 1856, and her childhood was that of a healthy, happy, country girl. At suitable age she was prepared for college in the public schools of Bloomington, entered the University of Indiana in 1872, and creditably completed the college classical curriculum in 1876. Contrary to custom among "sweet girl graduates"—in that day at least—she chose as her graduation exercise an oration rather than an essay—on the subject "What Woman May Do." After leaving college she taught in the public schools of the city until 1878, when she was married to James K. Beck, then superintendent of schools in Bloomington, and until recently associate professor of Latin in the University of Indiana.

Mrs. Beck when but a school-girl caught the crusade spirit and early took her p'ace with the W. C. T. U. of Indiana, serving it in various capacities until 1891, when she was called to the presidency. With her husband and five children Mrs. Beck has a pleasant and happy home, and is universally loved and respected by all who know her.

Mrs. Eva Ratcliff, of Vinita, Indian Territory, who succeeds Mrs. Stapler, as President of the Territorial W. C. T. U., is a Cherokee woman of influence and ability. She is of Presbyterian faith, zealous in church and Sunday-school work, and like many of our leaders, was for some years a teacher. In early womanhood she was married to Edgar N. Ratcliff, of Texas, and is the mother of five children. Mrs. Ratcliff thoroughly appreciates the sentiment expressed by Lady Henry Somerset: "She loves home most who knows best the dangers that lie outside." About four years ago she united with the W. C. T. U. and since that time has been a loyal and efficient worker.

Mrs. Marion B. Dunham, Burlington, President of Iowa, is a native of Ohio. She was a school teacher for many years, six of them in the public schools of Chicago, leaving there to marry C. A. Dunham, an architect of Burlington, Iowa, which city has since been her home. She began active temperance work in 1877, served as county and district president, and in 1884 was elected state superintendent of Scientific Temperance Instruction, securing the passage of the desired law in her second year of office. When the disaffection of the Iowa union began she remained firm and true to the National and its policy, and on the secession of the old union was elected to the presidency, and is now serving her fifth year. Both she and her husband are identified with the Prohibition party and she has served as candidate on the state ticket several times. Mrs. Dunham is a woman of chain-lightning celerity of mind and action, a leader well fitted to the difficult emergency of our work in that state.

Mrs. Lurenda Beverly Smith, President of Kansas, was born in New York, in 1844. A year later her parents settled in one of the now suburban towns of Chicago, and she received her education in the public schools of Cook county, Illinois. Later she attended a private school in Boston for two years, and in 1862 was married to Lieut. Malcolm F. Smith, of Cleveland. They removed to Kansas in 1868. Mrs. Smith has been a member of the W. C. T. U. eighteen years. Her help was given in securing the Prohibitory Amendment, and later, the Scientific Temperance Instruction Law, and also in raising funds for the support of the "Industrial School for Girls," which was started by the W. C. T. U., and afterwards became a state institution. She did effective work as state superintendent of work among colored people for two years, served seven years as president of the Second District, and since 1893, as state president.

Mrs. Margaret Anderson Watts, President of Kentucky, is the wife of Robert Augustine Watts, one of the most estimable citizens of the state. She is the daughter of Hon. S. H. Anderson, a lawyer and orator of distinction, who died while a member of Congress. On the maternal side she is the granddaughter of Judge William Owsley, the fourteenth governor of Kentucky. Her ancestor, the Rev. John Owsley, was in the seventeenth century rector of the Glouston Church of Leicestershire, England, for fifty years. She comes from an educated and talented stock and ample means gave her fine educational advantages. Mrs. Watts is a deep thinker on all advanced topics of the day and her views have been published in various papers. She was one of the first women of Kentucky who dared to advocate higher education and the ballot for women. She has been an active member of the W. C. T. U. for many years; has held the offices of National superintendent of

Police Matron work; state superintendent of Scientific Temperance Instruction; state corresponding secretary and state president, in each proving herself a faithful and efficient worker. Mrs. Watts was a member of the Woman's Auxiliary Board of the Parliament of Religions in 1893, and she is a charter member of the Woman's Club of her city, which club holds a prominent place in the Federation of Clubs.

Mrs. Mary Read Goodale, President of the Louisiana W. C. T. U., is the wife of Prof. Wilmot H. Goodale, of Louisiana State University. Her mother, Mrs. Mary W. Read, one of Louisiana's foremost educators, came from Wilbraham Seminary, Massachusetts, about 1835, to establish a girls' boarding school in Baton Rouge, where she taught for fifty years. Mrs. Goodale's connection with the W. C. T. U. began about the time of the Detroit Convention, in 1883, and since that time she has attended every National convention and two World's conventions. She has served the state in many official capacities and as National Organizer has traveled through the entire South. Mrs. Goodale is one of the surprises of this new crusade. A few years ago a quiet, retiring woman, frightened at the sound of her own voice when that voice was heard by a dozen auditors; now going from state to state addressing the largest audiences and thrilling them through and through. Nor has her public work detracted one iota from her sweet womanliness, as all who have enjoyed the hospitality of her beautiful home at Baton Rouge can testify.

Mrs. L. M. N. Stevens is President of Maine, also Vice-President of the National W. C. T. U. For sketch see page 20.

Mrs. Mary Haslup, Maryland's President, succeeded Mrs. Baldwin, who served the union so long and faithfully, in 1894, after having become well known in the state as Organizer, and as one of its vice-presidents. She is the widow of a minister; a woman of rare spiritual mind and of calm, even temperament; logical, unusually clear and direct in perception and expression, untiring in her devotion to duty, of which her standard is the highest, and most admirably adapted to the position to which her co-workers have called her. Maryland has been truly fortunate in her presidents. Mrs. Mary Whitall Thomas, the revered and beloved sister of Hannah Whitall Smith, Mrs. Baldwin, and now Mrs. Haslup.

MRS. SUSAN S. FESSENDEN.

Mrs. Susan S. Fessenden, of Boston, is a progressive thinker upon all lines of reform. She was born in Cincinnati, Ohio, but has resided in the East for the last ten years, with the exception of three years spent abroad. She has served as National Superintendent of the department of Franchise, and in 1890 was elected President of the Massachusetts Union. She is regarded as one of the most scholarly and statesmanlike speakers that the white-ribbon movement has produced. It is her good fortune to have something to say and to say it with clearness and conviction, wit and wisdom. Mrs. Fessenden has wonderful intellectual balance, combined with the most winning and womanly grace, and delights both the masculine and feminine auditors in any assembly of educated people.

Mrs. A. S. Benjamin, of Michigan, is one of our strongest women, and as a parliamentarian has made for herself a unique place in the National W. C. T. U. She is a graduate of Oberlin College and a teacher of high standing. As president of the Fifth Congressional District of Michigan, which position she has filled for sixteen consecutive years, she first gave evidence of her strength as a white-ribbon leader—having worked up that district so successfully that it is better systematized and equipped than many a state union we could mention. She has been National Superintendent of Parliamentary Usage eight years, of Schools of Methods two years, and since the death of Mrs. Lathrap, president of the state. Mrs. Benjamin is a gifted speaker and has lectured on various lines of the temperance reform in many states. Her parliamentary drills given at Chautauqua and other summer assemblies are full of interest and instruction, brightened by her own exhaustless humor, and she is in great demand at conventions and summer assemblies. It is no easy task to fill the place occupied by our " Daniel Webster " for so long, but in calling Mrs. Benjamin to its presidency Michigan W. C. T. U. has chosen wisely and well.

Mrs. Susanna M. D. Fry, whom Minnesota W. C. T. U. has recently called to the Presidency, was reared on a farm in Ohio, graduated from the Western Female Seminary at Oxford, and was a teacher in the grammar and high schools of the state. In 1868 she was married to Rev. James D. Fry, a graduate of the Ohio Wesleyan University, and later spent two years in European travel, becoming a regular correspondent for several papers and a contributor to various literary periodicals. In 1876 she was elected to the chair of Belles-lettres in the Illinois University, which position she occupied until 1890. In 1878 she received from the Ohio University the degree of A. M. and later from the Syracuse University that of Ph. D. After removing to St. Paul she became connected with the State University of Minnesota, and in 1893 was elected a judge in the Liberal Arts department of the Columbian Exposition. Mrs. Fry early identified herself with the W. C. T. U. movement, and in 1879, when the home protection petition was presented to the legislature of Illinois was one of the spokeswomen of the committee. She has been president of a number of important organizations and has made many addresses before various conferences on moral, educational and temperance topics.

Mrs. Clara C. Hoffman is Missouri's white-ribbon leader. For sketch see page 23.

Mrs. Lavinia S. Mount, President of Mississippi, was born in Vicksburg. She is a direct descendent of Richard Stockton, one of the signers of the Declaration of Independence, and Annis Boudinot, of Huguenot lineage. Her father, Marmaduke Shannon, played a prominent part in overthrowing the lawlessness which characterized the early days of Vicksburg. Mrs. Mount's career, though quiet, as accords with the modesty of her character, is worthy of her blood. Her first temperance work was with the "Friends of Temperance." When a W. C. T. U. was organized in Vicksburg in 1886, she was elected one of its officers. In 1887 she became state recording secretary and in 1888 state president. Her husband, Thomas Mount, was the candidate of the Prohibition party for Congress from his district in the last election. He is in full accord with his wife's temperance work and both take an advanced position on the "woman question." Both are members of the Methodist Church South, and active church workers.

Mrs. Mary B. Wylie, President Montana W. C. T. U., was born and educated in Iowa. She taught school three years and was married in 1874 to W. W. Wylie, then principal of school at Delhi, Iowa. In 1879 they removed to Montana, Mr. Wylie taking charge of the schools at Bozeman. Mrs. Wylie knows much of the pioneer life of the far West, and before the days of railroads in Montana has many times traveled by stage five hundred miles at a stretch over mountains and canons. She has been prominently identified with the temperance work in that state for many years, was delegate to the National W. C. T. U. Convention at Boston in 1891, and was called to the state presidency in 1894. Mrs. Wylie is a woman of energetic spirit, vigorous physique and impressive manner and is making for herself a praiseworthy record as one of the newer leaders in the W. C. T. U.

Mrs. S. M. Walker's election as State President of Nebraska was in the line of "natural evolution." As local and district president she displayed those qualities of leadership which inevitably bring promotion. Among these is the rare gift of harmonizing discordant elements, which, united with a radical aggressiveness in all departments of W. C. T. U. work is one of Mrs. Walker's chief characteristics. She possesses power, in a remarkable degree, to draw out the latent talents of timid and self-depreciating workers. President for many years of Nebraska's famous Fourth District and vice-president of the state under Mrs. Hitchcock, Mrs. Walker is evidently the right woman in the right place.

Mrs. Lucy M. Van Deventer, President of the Nevada W. C. T. U., is the wife of Rev. Dr. E. W. Van Deventer, superintendent of the Nevada mission of the M. E. church. She is a native of Illinois, graduated from Hedding College, and was a white-ribbon worker in Kansas during the great victorious struggle for constitutional prohibition. She was state president of Nevada for five consecutive years and is now serving her sixth term, being again elected after an interim of two years.

Miss C. R. Wendell, New Hampshire's President, was born in Dover, New Hampshire, where she now resides. She comes from an old Dutch family, the Wendells being, contemporary with the Knickerbocker families of New York. From her mother, a woman of remarkable strength of character, she inherited a love for benevolent and reform movements. For thirteen years she was corresponding secretary of the New Hampshire W. C. T. U., devoting herself with untiring vigilance to the advancement of the organization, and in 1892 was elected president of the state. Miss Wendell is an active member of several philanthropic societies, a thorough believer in equal suffrage, and is ready to aid any cause that has for its object the upbuilding of mankind.

Mrs. Emma Bourne, President of the New Jersey W. C. T. U. since 1891, was born in Newark, New Jersey, of Scottish Huguenot ancestry; her father coming in boyhood from England to this country. Her mother is known to white-ribboners as "Mother Hill." She was educated at the Newark Wesleyan Institute, receiving also a diploma from the Newark Normal School; taught seven years; married in 1868 and spent four years abroad. Mrs. Bourne was for seven years president of the first W. C. T. U. organized in New Jersey at Newark and has attended all the National Conventions. Since 1874 she has served in the Newark union as recording secretary, superintendent of L. T. L., Literature and the Press; was recording secretary of Essex county until elected president of the state; organized New Jersey's department of Literature, and was its recording secretary for ten years previous to taking her present office.

Rev. Mary J. Borden, for five years President of New Mexico W. C. T. U., is an ordained minister of the Congregational church, an indefatigable and zealous worker in every good cause. She wins the heart by her unswerving loyalty to the principles of right, her unselfish devotion and her earnest, pleading eloquence as a public speaker. Almost her entire time is devoted to public work. A Kentuckian by birth, in early childhood Michigan became her home by adoption. Her family consists of her husband, two daughters and a son, all devoted Christian workers. Mrs. Borden is also president of the New Mexico Orphans' Home, a benevolent institution for homeless children sustained by territorial appropriations. During the last legislative assembly this busy woman secured the passage of a law prohibiting the sale of tobacco in any form to minors in New Mexico. Thus shall the children of that territory rise up and call her blessed.

Mrs. Mary Towne Burt, for many years President of the W. C. T. U. of New York, is a marked figure in all white-ribbon circles. She is the daughter of a former rector of the Church of England; was born in Ohio; removed to Auburn, New York, with her widowed mother when twelve years old; was educated in the public schools and in the Auburn Young Ladies' Institute and four years after leaving school was married to Edward Burt. She dates her awakening to the world's needs to the crusade fire of 1874, which swept her from her home of ease and elegance into the unceasing round of toil she has since

MRS. MARY T. BURT.

known. She was one of the secretaries of the first National Council, and later became National corresponding secretary. Queenly in presence, courtly in speech, elegant in manners in private life as well as dignified aud inspiring in public, Mrs. Burt is well fitted to lead the more than twenty thousand women of the great Empire State whose motto is "Excelsior." She has a pleasant home in upper New York City with her husband and son who are heartily in sympathy with her.

Mrs. Henrietta L. Monroe, Ohio's loved and honored President, is a native of that state, one of the original crusaders, and a pioneer leader in the W. C. T. U. Her father was Zachariah Riley, a lawyer and a gentleman of the old school; her mother was granddaughter of a Revolutionary Captain in Virginia and cousin of "Stonewall" Jackson. Mrs. Monroe had the advantage of a total abstinence training and even in her school days was member of a temperance organization. In 1848 she was married to Mr. James B. Monroe of Xenia, a cultured Christian business man who is interested equally with his wife in all reform work. Reared in a conservative communion, the United Presbyterian, it was no easy matter for her to lead a crusade procession on the streets, but the movement came to her as the voice of God, enlisting all her sympathies and developing a talent for leadership which her friends quickly recognized. From that time she has devoted her life to W. C. T. U. work, and in 1886 was called to the state presidency. Her clear judgment and resourceful mind, seconded by a corps of loyal and efficient workers, has placed Ohio in the front rank as a W. C. T. U. state. Six sons and daughters have blessed her home, which has been an ideal one, for she is in the largest sense a homekeeper. Her family holds a leading place in Xenia in every particular. As one of Mrs. Monroe's loyal constituency says of her: "No state has greater reason to be proud of her representative, both at home and in the National, than Ohio."

Mrs. Marinda Bull Switzer, President of Oklahoma Territory, is a native of Ohio. She graduated from the Ohio Wesleyan Female Colege in 1866; went with her parents to Nebraska in 1870 and there became a crusade leader. She was married in 1876 to Mr. S. W. Switzer. Her first platform work was done in 1881 during the equal suffrage amendment campaign in that state. Both Mr. and Mrs. Switzer did valiant service for the cause and their pleasant home in Bloomington, where Mr. Switzer was at that time Register of the Land Office, was always open to the workers and speakers. When defeat came, realizing that it was largely due to the influence of the liquor power, she cast in her lot with its most powerful foe, and since that time has been a tireless worker in the W. C. T. U., first in Nebraska, then in California, and for the last three years in Oklahoma where she is a pillar of strength to the work. She is now serving her second term as president of the territory.

Mrs. Narcissa White=Kinney, President of Oregon W. C. T. U., well known in the East in teachers' institutes and temperance circles as Narcissa White, is a native of Pennsylvania. In 1886 she was sent by the National Union to the Pacific coast to aid in securing scientific temperance and prohibition legislation, and two years later returned to Oregon as the wife of Mr. Kinney, a prominent business man of Astoria. For four years she has been the general secretary of the state Chautauqua Association and for one year editor of *The Chautauquan*. Three Chautauqua assemblies in the state show the result of her efforts. In connection with the president of the State University and the state superintendent of Public Instruction, she is one of the directors and founders of the seaside "Summer School for Teachers." Mrs. Kinney is a very impressive public speaker, and possesses the instincts of a born leader. What has been Pennsylvania's loss is Oregon's gain.

Mrs. Anna M. H. Lawton Hammer, President of Pennsylvania, is a native of that state, born in Pottsville, Schuylkill county, and educated in Wilkes-Barre and Philadelphia, in which latter city she was married to William Alexander Hammer, in 1862. She comes of Revolutionary stock, two of her great-grandfathers being generals in the army, and her great-grandfather Lawton, a surgeon, stationed at West Point. Her maternal grandfather was an officer in the Navy in the war of 1812, and was wounded in the engagement of the *Chesapeake* and *Shannon*, under Captain Lawrence, the latter Commander being a cousin on the Lawton side. With this historic record, it is not remarkable that Anna M. Hammer should be imbued with love of country and be ready for active warfare against this foe of her native land, the liquor traffic. She has been in the work twenty years, sixteen of which she has been a National superintendent. She is serving her third term as president of her native state, and is committed for God and Home and Every Land.

Mrs. Mary Adaline Babcock, President of Rhode Island, graduated from the public school and began teaching at seventeen years of age. In 1860 she entered the Female Seminary at Troy, New York, founded by Mrs. Emma Willard, from which institution she graduated in 1862, sharing with one other the highest honors of a large class. Since her marriage in 1866 to Daniel Babcock, her home has been in Phœnix, Rhode Island, and she has been closely identified with the educational and religious interests of the state. In the summer of 1883 she joined the local W. C. T. U. and soon became one of the most earnest and enthusiastic workers of the state. In the delicate and difficult work of the Social Purity department of her state she has proved herself a leader of rare ability and discretion, her addresses before public audiences and before the legislature always being attended with marked results. In 1890 Mrs. Babcock was made state president, and since that time has given herself unreservedly to the work, always loyally carrying out the plans of the National Union, never grudging time or strength for the advancement of our cause, and always an example of unselfishness and high integrity.

Mrs. Lide Meriwether has for the past ten years led the white-ribbon host in Tennessee. A woman of rare courage, earnestness of conviction, catholicity of sympathies, she has led her devoted followers on step by step, until now the W. C. T. U. of Tennessee stands side by side with the National on all leading issues. Throughout her useful life of sixty-five years Mrs. Meriwether has stood as the staunch friend of woman, her most salient characteristic being absolute fearlessness where a principle is involved. Thirty years ago she put forth a modest volume entitled "Soundings," which was a simple, earnest plea for a "white life for two," and this at a time when no pure woman, in the South at least, dared touch the social question. As a writer of both prose and poetry, her style is clear, pointed and graceful, and as a platform speaker her chief characteristics are a resistless logic and the charm of a strong magnetic personality.

Mrs. Helen M. Stoddard, W. C. T. U. leader in Texas, first saw the light in a frontier cabin in the forests of Wisconsin. Her early education was gained partly in the little country schoolhouse, partly in the big "sitting room" at home. Part of the year 1860 was spent in Ripon College, preparatory to teaching her first school. Later she entered

Genesee Wesleyan Seminary, at Lima, New York, and in 1873 graduated with valedictory honors in a large class. She was married two years after to Mr. S. D. Stoddard, of New York, and was widowed in 1878, the mother of two boys. She resumed teaching; resigning her last position —in Fort Worth University—to accept the presidency of the W. C. T. U, which office she has held since 1891. Mrs. Stoddard has carried the gospel of the white-ribbon to the remotest corners of this immense state; was instrumental in securing the Scientific Temperance Instruction Law for Texas in 1893. and has spent the winter of '95 at the capital in the interest of a better "Age of Consent" law, an anti-tobacco law, and other progressive legislation. She is delegate from her state to the World's Convention in London.

Mrs. G. W. Martin, W. C. T. U. leader in Utah, is of Ohio birth, but for sixteen years has lived in Manti, Utah, her present home. Her labors in the missionary cause revealed to her the need of temperance work in the territory. and when one of our National organizers, Mrs. Reese, visited Utah, Mrs. Martin becoming convinced that W. C. T. U. methods were admirably suited to the conditions of the territory, took up its lines of work with alacrity, and ever since has been, in the face of great difficulties, faithfully, if quietly, pushing forward the white-ribbon gospel in Utah.

Mrs. Ida B. Read, President of Vermont W. C. T. U., was born April 3, 1844, in Luzerne, New York, where her early childhood was passed. Her wide experience as a teacher, both in the public school and Sabbath-school greatly aided in the development of a natural gift of keen insight into character. She was for several years actively engaged in the Home and Foreign Mission work of the Methodist Episcopal church. Mrs. Read possesses an amiable disposition, sound judgment and great executive ability. As a public speaker her earnestness and enthusiasm charm all who listen to her. Her manner is pleasing and her words full of the practical truth which carries conviction. Her husband and daughter are in full sympathy with her work and aid her in every way possible in her service for God and humanity.

Mrs. R. B. Jones, of Norfolk, Virginia, was born in North Carolina, in 1841. Her father was for fifty years a Methodist minister, and Mrs. Jones has been a member of that church from childhood. She was made President of the W. C. T. U. of Virginia, in 1889, and manages to fill that position with great satisfaction to her constituency without neglecting any of the numerous family duties which fall to her share. She is active in district and local work and a leader in church and missionary organizations; is president of the Florence Crittenton Home, which she projected; president of the City Orphan Asylum and a member of the board of managers of the Retreat for the Sick. In fact her life is one round of consecrated work for the Master. Six years ago too timid to preside at her first convention, Mrs. Jones is to-day making telling speeches for temperance throughout her state.

Mrs. H. R. C. Morrow is President of West Virginia. The first thirteen years of her life were spent at the place of her birth on a farm in Hancock county, West Virginia. She received from Presbyterian parents, of Scotch-Irish lineage, careful religious training, and united at the age of fifteen with the Presbyterian church; entered the public schools of New Cumberland as teacher when sixteen years of age, teaching there several years and at the same time diligently pursuing a course of study. She resigned her position to enter Beaver College, Pennsylvania, from which institution she graduated in 1880, subsequently receiving the honorary degree of A. M. She resumed teaching and in 1882 received an appointment as teacher in the State Normal School of Fairmont, West Virginia. Five of the nine years in that school she was assistant principal, the ninth year principal. She resigned to spend some time in travel abroad, and later was married in New York city to George Morrow. She was elected to her present office June, '94, having been for two years state secretary of Y work, and for seven years president of the local union of Fairmont. Mrs. Morrow is ably seconded in her work by her husband who is an uncompromising Prohibitionist and a ruling elder in the Presbyterian church. To his sympathy and hearty encouragement much of her success is due.

Mrs. Delle T. Cox, President of East Washington, was born in Illinois in 1853, and at the age of seventeen went to Kansas, where she taught for some years, marrying A. C. Cox in 1874. She took part in the campaign for prohibition in that state and held offices in local, county, district and state unions until her removal to Oregon in 1891. The next year she was elected National Organizer, which office she still retains. Upon her election to the office of state president, Mrs. Cox removed to Ellensburg where she now resides and is making earnest effort to place the W. C. T. U. of that state upon a footing worthy that great commonwealth of rare natural beauty.

Mrs. Ella J. Fifield, M. D., of West Washington, was born in Wisconsin. She early removed to Minnesota where she was educated in the public schools, and fitted for a teacher in the Mankato Normal school. She spent six years in teaching and during that time removed to California where she became interested in the study of medicine, and in 1883 graduated from Cooper Medical College, of San Francisco. Previous to this time she married Dr. W. E. Fifield, who has always been heartily in sympathy with her both in her medical and temperance work. Mrs. Fifield's first W. C. T. U. work was in Petaluma, California, where she was president of the local union. On her removal to Tacoma. Washington, she was made president of Tacoma Central union, and in June, 1894, was elected state president.

Mrs. Vie H. Campbell was elected to the Presidency of the Wisconsin W. C. T. U. in June 1892, and has been twice re-elected. She is of Quaker ancestry and Wisconsin birth and much of her life has been spent in her native state. She was among the earliest workers in the Wisconsin Union, and helped to mold the enthusiasm of the woman's revolt against the saloon into a systematic working force. Mrs. Campbell as president of the First Congressional District was a model officer. To unusual gifts as a public speaker she added a quick sympathy, temperate judgment, broad charity and remarkable executive ability, and brought every union in the district into sympathetic touch with herself and each other. Her later work in the state is but an enlargement of her former work in the district. Although complicated by the difficulties involved in a larger constituency, the work of the State W. C. T. U. is under her administration carried on in the same spirit of independent thought, earnest endeavor and Christian charity.

Mrs. Wilhelmina Brown (*née* Fillmore), President of Wyoming, is one of the pioneers of the West. She is a near relative of United States President Fillmore, was born in the state of New York in 1854 and removed to Wyoming when sixteen years of age. She has been in W. C. T. U. work eleven years, being, as she says, one of Miss Willard's personal converts. Her husband is a prominent lawyer, a pronounced advocate of woman's suffrage, and was president of the state convention which indorsed that measure four years ago.

SUPERINTENDENTS.

For sketch of Mrs. Frances J. Barnes, General Secretary of Young Woman's Branch, see page 9.

Mrs. Emma L. Evans, of New York, was appointed Department Secretary of Y. W. C. T. U. work, by the National Union in 1882, and since the department was changed to a Branch has continued the service as its "good right-hand." She was born near Philadelphia, of Quaker parents; was educated at the Friends School and at the well-known private school of Mary Anna Longstreth. To other benevolent organizations, as well as to the W. C. T. U., Mrs. Evans gives of her time and influence; among them the National Christian League for the promotion of Social Purity and the old and honored institution known as the Female Guardian Society and Home for the Friendless, in the industrial school of which she has introduced a weekly temperance lesson. Mrs. Evans combines the tact and grace of a charming personality with the wisdom and practical business ability of a woman of affairs. She is lovingly spoken of by the Y's as their "Model Secretary."

Mrs. Helen G. Rice, of Boston, Massachusetts, is our Superintendent of Juvenile work. No woman enters upon her work with a more whole-souled enthusiasm, or brings to it greater versatility and originality than does this commander-in-chief of the Loyal Temperance Legion. A happy wife in a childless home, her innate love for children has found its proper channel, and in a truer sense than can be said of many homes, she "mothers" the childhood of the nation. Under her wise planning, for five years, the work of the L. T. L. has broadened and deepened, until it has become indeed the reserve corps of the temperance army. Mrs. Rice is recording secretary for the Massachusetts W. C. T. U., a fine speaker to both children and adults, and among the most valued of New England white-ribboners.

Mrs. Sophie F. Grubb, of Kirkwood, Missouri, has been for twelve years at the head of W. C. T. U. work for foreign-speaking peoples in this country. She comes of a family of exceptionally gifted women, and was formerly devoted to literary studies, but for many years past has given her entire time and not a little money to developing her department. She issues leaflets in eighteen languages on almost any subject connected with our many-sided work. She never abuses, never antagonizes, aiming first to secure the good-will and then the intellectual concurrence of those who come from distant countries. Mrs. Grubb is one of our best speakers and most devoted workers. Her assistant in the Scandinavian is Miss Kate Lunden, of New Jersey. In the Dutch, Mrs. Van Olinda, of Holland, Mich.; Mrs. E. J. Harwood, of New Mexico, for the Spanish, and Mrs. Nellie B. Eyster, of California, for the Chinese.

Mrs. Lucy Thurman, Superintendent of Work among Colored People, has been talking for temperance ever since crusade days. She was born near Toronto, Canada, in 1852. Even as a child her love for oratory was so pronounced that she would climb the hills and address mimic audiences. She left home when seventeen, determined to do something for the elevation of her race. She taught a school in Maryland for three years and then went to Jackson, Michigan, where she married. Mrs. Thurman has lectured in both Southern and Northern States, her audiences being more often white than colored. She is state superintendent of Colored work in Michigan, district superintendent of Evangelistic work, and president of Jackson county W. C. T. U. The Thurmans have a beautiful home in Jackson where they have entertained many distinguished persons. Frederick Douglass was for twenty-six years a warm friend of the family.

Dr. Annette Shaw, of the department of Health and Heredity, is vice-president of the Wisconsin W. C. T. U. and state superintendent of Social Purity and Legislative work, and no more fitting leader could be found for this important branch of preventive work. She comes of sterling New England ancestry; is a graduate of St. Lawrence University, New York, and was ordained a minister in the Universalist church. After eight years of pastorate, a throat difficulty developed which necessitated a rest from preaching. She then took a course in medicine. Unselfish and unostentatious in all she does, Dr. Shaw devotes her life largely to philanthropic work, and the W. C. T. U. Home for Erring Girls at Eau Claire is one of the results of her untiring work and self-sacrifice.

Mrs. Abbie E. Shapleigh, Superintendent of the department which aims to teach Scientific and Economic Cookery, is a native of Maine. With an ancestry on either side of industrious patriotic people and with parents who were much in advance of their time in liberal thought and temperance principles, the children could hardly fail to develop strength of character and moral fiber. Mrs. Shapleigh has been known for many years as a faithful worker in the white-ribbon cause, her interest centering mainly in the departments that aim to prevent and forestall the evils of strong drink. Believing that wrong can best be eradicated by incorporating the right, she holds that the proper food for the body would prevent the desire either for strong drink or for any injurious stimulant.

For sketch of Mrs. Mary H. Hunt, Superintendent of Scientific Temperance Instruction, see page 10.

Mrs. Frances Wait Leiter, Superintendent of Physical Culture, one of Ohio's gifted daughters, has given twenty-one years of faithful service to the cause of humanity; local, state and National departments having felt the vitalizing touch of her influence. Well devised plans ably carried out, and her arguments before the legislature secured Ohio's Temperance Education law. A successful educator in former years and now a successful wife and mother in a beautiful home she finds time and zeal to help in the general home-brightening of the country. She ranks high as a lecturer before colleges, teachers' institutes and woman's clubs. In her official capacity it is Mrs. Leiter's aim to secure state laws requiring physical training in the public schools.

Mrs. Stella Blanchard Irvine, Superintendent of Sunday-school work, was born and educated in Wisconsin; was a teacher in the public schools of La Crosse, and was married in 1882 to Mr. Lew W. Irvine, of St. Paul, Minnesota. Naturally of a religious turn of mind, her chosen field was the Sunday-school, in which work she soon won honor and distinction. She became a member of the W. C. T. U. in 1884, has since worked with that organization in various capacities, local, county, district and state, and has proved herself a "born leader." Through the ministry of affliction she heard the divine call to work for the safety of Christ's little ones and finds a most acceptable field in the Sunday-school department of the W. C. T. U.

For sketch of Mrs. Katherine Lente Stevenson, Superintendent of Temperance Literature, see page 21.

Mrs. S. E. V. Emery, of the department of the Relation of Temperance to Capital and Labor, is one of those tireless workers whose name has echoed throughout the land. As early as 1868, when reform movements were in their infancy, Mrs. Emery began writing upon temperance and suffrage. In 1880 she became interested in financial reform and since that time that subject has been her specialty. Mrs. Emery's published works, "Seven Financial Conspiracies" and "Imperialism in America," have had a phenomenal sale, and the *Corner-Stone*, an eight-page monthly started in 1893, already has a circulation in nearly every state and territory.

Miss Lodie Reed, Superintendent of Press work, has been one of the greatest factors in the work of the W. C. T. U. of Indiana, from the beginning. Born in Urbana, Ohio, she received a college education, attaining to an A. M. degree and afterward studying law with her father. In the winter of 1873-74, visiting in her native town she became fired with the crusade spirit. Already an earnest Christian, thenceforward her life-work was fixed and her lot cast with the women who prayed and fought against the liquor traffic. Being established in Indiana as a teacher, she was made state W. C. T. U. corresponding secretary, an office which she filled for thirteen years, with the fidelity only possible in a nature of such complete consecration as hers, finally declining renomination in 1894. She was one of the founders of the Indiana W. C. T. U. paper, *The Organizer*, and has been its editor for twelve years. Her fine discrimination and grasp of the needs of the work, called her to the broader field of National Press superintendent and editor of the *National W. C. T. U. Bulletin*. With four 'years' intermission, Miss Reed has served her state as superintendent of the Scientific Temperance Instruction department since it was adopted, in 1881, and under her generalship the "black cap" was removed from Indiana in 1894.

Mrs. E. B. Ingalls, of St. Louis, Missouri, Superintendent of the department of Narcotics, is perhaps the most attractive apostle that the anti-tobacco crusade has developed. She is the daughter of a very liberal-minded mother, has been a temperance worker from girlhood, a member of the W. C. T. U. since its first organization in her city, and for years the financier of the state organization. She is president of the St. Louis District Union and delegate to the World's Convention in London. As National superintendent her work is continuous and thorough, and many states' have enacted laws forbidding the sale of tobacco or cigarettes to minors. Mrs. Ingalls is popular in society and at all social gatherings wears her knot of white ribbon. Her husband supports her in all her endeavors and is proud of her ability as a leader.

For sketch of Miss Elizabeth Greenwood, Superintendent of the Evangelistic department, see page 11.

Miss Mary Moore is Superintendent of the department which aims to secure Unfermented Sacramental Wine. Her father was a pioneer in the temperance cause in western New York. Miss Moore was graduated from the Clover Street Seminary, Brighton, New York, an institution founded by her father, and under the principalship of her aunt. For twelve years she was principal of a private school, and afterwards taught in Lake Forest University, Illinois, leaving her position there for a year's travel abroad. In 1890 Miss Moore commenced active work in the W. C. T. U., of which organization she had long been a member, as superintendent of Scientific Temperance Instruction for Wyoming county, New York, and at the National Convention at Cleveland was appointed to her present office.

Mrs. Jane M. Kinney, Superintendent of Penal and Reformatory work, comes on the father's side from the pioneer settlers of Pennsylvania and New York, and on the mother's from McCallum More, of the famous Scotch Clan, Campbell. Widowed when quite young and her only child being taken away when five years old, Mrs. Kinney's heart turned instinctively to the sorrowing of every class, and the crusade found her ready to answer its call. She has been ever since a tireless worker in many lines of W. C. T. U. work in local, district and state unions. Her sympathies and her efforts are not limited to the white-ribbon organization. We cannot begin to tell of other activities which make her one of the busiest of reformers.

Mrs. S. A. Morrison, Superintendent of Almshouse work, is a great-granddaughter of General John Swift, a Revolutionary soldier and a granddaughter of Rev. Marcus Swift, a pioneer of Wayne county, Michigan, whose home was a station on the famous underground railroad of slavery days. Reared under such influences, Mrs. Morrison did not hesitate to unite with any reform movement, and has been identified with the W. C. T. U. since the days of the crusade. She began her almshouse work ten years ago in the Detroit poorhouse. Having been in constant touch with extended local work of this department in her own state of Michigan, she has had opportunity to study its many phases and needs and is well fitted in every way to be our National leader in this outreaching work.

Mrs. Margaret D. W. Merrill is at the head of the department for Securing Homes for Homeless Children. She is of old English ancestry and of New England birth. "Threescore and ten, and yet eight more," her Homes have been in Massachusetts, Maryland, New York and Maine. Asked why she has given unwavering fealty to the Woman's Christian Temperance Union, through its twenty years of "praise and blame," her reply is given in the words of a noble forerunner of Miss Willard, "Because I am a woman, and nothing concerning the interests of women and children is alien to me." Among Mrs. Merrill's efforts in the service of humanity are those in behalf of the Industrial Schools for Girls, the Temporary Home for women and children, and in conjunction with these, for homeless and dependent children.

Mrs. Caroline M. Clark=Woodward, who has charge of the work among Railroad Employés, was born on a Wisconsin farm, was educated in Milwaukee and afterward taught in that city. Of intelligent, energetic parentage, the daughter inherited the pioneer instinct and spirit, with genius for organization. She was a general officer of Nebraska W. C. T. U. nine years; was appointed National organizer in 1887; associate of department of work among Railroad Employés in 1890; and elected National Superintendent in 1892. She received Prohibition party nominations for Regent of the Nebraska University and for Member of Congress. Mrs. Woodward studied "Methods" under Mary Allen West at Lake Bluff and Chicago schools and has since conducted schools of Methods at various Chautauqua Assemblies. She is a clear and forcible speaker, a skillful parliamentarian, and is one of our most workmanlike leaders.

Mrs. Sarah A. McClees has for twelve years worked for sobriety and purity in the Army and Navy of the United States. Her effort to suppress the "canteen system" by petition and memorial to Congress is a historical incident of great importance. Her latest success has been the placing of temperance libraries on board our war cruisers and merchant ships. Sojourning temporarily in California, she is establishing the same network of influences on the Pacific Coast. Aiding the W. C. T. U. as one of their representatives in the Federation of Societies, as an executive officer in the Equal Suffrage Association and the Southern California Woman's Press Club, her sphere of usefulness is widely extended. Crusade days found Mrs. McClees in New York City remonstrating with saloon-keepers ; secretary of the first union, afterwards its president and for five years president of Westchester county, New York.

Mrs. Mary C. Upham, who holds the Superintendency of work in Lumber Camps, is the wife of the present governor of Wisconsin. She is, on her mother's side, of Quaker descent; was married to Major Upham in 1867 and for many years lived in the pine forests of northern Wisconsin, where she first became aroused to the need of work among the camps. She inaugurated a systematic plan for supplying them with good literature by mail from hundreds of homes. This plan was productive of such good results that it was afterwards adopted by other states. In Mrs. Upham's own words, her work is "based upon the fact that the divine influence which prompts one woman to do good ever finds sympathy in the hearts of all good women of the white ribbon army."

Mrs. Winnie F. Minear English, Superintendent of Work among Miners, is a native of Illinois and has been from childhood a pronounced advocate of total abstinence. The daughter of a minister and physician, she had opportunity to learn of the destructive effects of the liquor traffic, and very early cast her voice and influence against the curse. For twenty-five years she has been the wife of an itinerant minister of the M. E. church, her husband now being a presiding elder in the Illinois Conference. In 1887, when the Illinois W. C. T. U. created the department of Work among Miners, Mrs. English was made the superintendent, and in 1891 National leader of the work. Under her direction the department has so rapidly developed that twenty-five states are now carrying forward this important branch of W. C. T. U. effort.

Mrs. Josephine C. Bateham, of the department of Sabbath Observance, is of New England parentage, brought up and educated at Oberlin, Ohio. She married Rev. R. Cushman and went with him as missionary to Hayti. Here she lost her husband, and returned home before she was twenty. She afterward married M. B. Bateham, an eminent horticulturist and writer, and lived in Ohio. For many years her life was largely devoted to her family of seven children, and especially to a gifted invalid daughter who died in 1885. Mrs. Bateham has lectured all over the country; has traveled extensively in Europe, the West Indies and Hawaii, and has published scores of leaflets, pamphlets and books.

Mrs. Mary F. Lovell, of Bryn Mawr, Pennsylvania, Superintendent of the Mercy department, is of English birth and parentage, but has spent nearly all her life in America. Her early training was such as to foster literary and artistic taste and high moral aims, and the education of the heart as well as the intellect has ever been her ideal of human development. She married early, but having no children has had opportunity for activity in various philanthropies and reforms, and to these has devoted years of earnest attention. Her chief work, however, is the effort to aid in developing in the human mind the idea of the obligations of mercy toward all God's creatures; also securing the enactment and enforcement of laws for this beneficent purpose. Mrs. Lovell is a woman of unusual refinement and education and has been for many years a leader in the Pennsylvania W. C. T. U.

Dr. Mary Wood=Allen, of our Purity department, was born in Delta, Ohio, in 1841; began teaching school at fourteen years of age, and teaching music at fifteen; entered the classical department of the College at Delaware, Ohio, in 1858; was graduated therefrom in 1861; married in 1863, and spent the years from 1871 to '74, in Europe, in travel and study. She received the degree of M. D. from the regular department of medicine of the University of Michigan, in 1875; was appointed National lecturer of the W. C. T. U. in Heredity and Hygiene, in 1885, and superintendent of the Purity department in 1892. Dr. Allen is an indefatigable worker and has published several books in the interests of her department, among which are: "The Man Wonderful in the House Beautiful," "Teaching Truth," "Child Confidence Rewarded," and "Almost a Man." She has recently started "The Mother's Friend," a monthly periodical designed to arouse the mother-thought on the vital question of purity.

Mrs. Emilie D. Martin, of New York, Superintendent of the department for Purity in Literature and Art, the daughter of a distinguished physician, who was at one time a leading abolitionist. She is a prominent Chautauquan and has been president for three years of the Guild of the Seven Seals. She is active in church work and is the New York synodical secretary of literature; was associated with Miss Willard in the promotion of Purity in Literature and Art, and chosen National Superintendent in 1891. Her husband is a prominent business man and is in entire sympathy with all Mrs. Martin's efforts.

Mrs. Mary D. Tomlinson, Superintendent of Parlor Meetings, was educated at Alford, University, New York, and the State Normal School in New Jersey, and like so many white-ribboners, was a successful teacher for some years. She married Dr. T. H. Tomlinson in 1868; in 1884 became actively engaged in W. C. T. U. work; was for nine years president of the local union at Plainfield; in 1886, chosen president of Union county W. C. T. U.; seven years state superintendent of Parlor Meetings; two years associate National superintendent of this department, and elected National superintendent in 1893. During all these years Mrs. Tomlinson has spent almost her entire time in work connected with our organization and is one of its most valued specialists.

Miss Alice L. Sudduth, of Colton, California, is Superintendent of one of the most popular and beautiful departments of white-ribbon work. Her own home in Southern California a bower of tropical beauty, she is well fitted by surroundings and an enthusiastic nature to direct the Flower Mission work of the National W. C. T. U., as for five years she has that of her state. Miss Sudduth was devoted to Miss Jennie Casseday, the founder and for fifteen years the invalid superintendent of this department, and her great endeavor is to perpetuate Miss Casseday's plans and purposes. She has arranged for many delightful substitutes for flowers, when the latter cannot be obtained.

Mrs. Clara V. Weaver is National Superintendent of State and County Fairs, and we are truly sorry that as these pages go to press the solicited sketch has not arrived.

Mrs. M. B. Ellis, the new Superintendent of Legislation and Petitions, is corresponding secretary of New Jersey and began her temperance career in California during the crusade. In state work she was closely associated with our "Andrew Jackson," Mrs. Downs, who said of her: "I never called Margaret Ellis to any place, great or small, where she did not come up to its requirements; you can trust her anywhere." A great, tender heart filled with the Christ-love, a natural gift of eloquence and a rich, musical voice—such are the characteristics which distinguish this daughter of New Jersey.

Mrs. L. C. Purington, M. D., leader of the Franchise department, is an all-round woman. A graduate of Mount Holyoke Seminary, of Hahnemann Medical College, and a life-long student in the school of experience, nothing that concerns humanity is foreign to her interest. Born into the kingdom of equal rights and inheriting stanch temperance principles, her fine executive and literary ability has been largely devoted to the elevation of woman, through the twin philanthropies—missions and temperance. She was a member of the Chicago W. C. T. U. at its start, and the first Y Union was formed at her house in Chicago. During the last ten years her residence at Dorchester, Massachusetts, has been marked by "labors abundant" in every good cause.

For sketch of Mrs. Hannah J. Bailey, Superintendent of Peace and Arbitration, see page 14.

ORGANIZERS.

Mrs. Helen Louise Bullock, born in Norwich, New York, early chose as her life-work the teaching of instrumental music, and studied with the best masters in New York City. She taught successfully for more than thirty years, publishing during that time a set of musical studies and a musical catechism. In 1886 a mysterious chain of circumstances, in which she recognized the voice of God, called her from her loved profession into the organizing work of the W. C. T. U. of her native state. Manifesting a peculiar fitness for this work she was in 1895 appointed National Organizer and has proved herself without a superior as an organizer of local unions. Mrs. Bullock is also one of our most cogent public speakers, her treatment of the tobacco question especially being unexcelled. She does not abuse or alienate, but simply holds up the mirror to nature's face. Her work has been signally blessed from the Atlantic to the Pacific.

Mrs. Lucy b. Washington, of Port Jervis, New York, is the wife of a Baptist minister and a graduate of Clover Street Seminary, Rochester, New York. She became one of the leaders of the crusade in Jacksonville, Illinois, and was at once brought into notice as a public speaker, her bright intellect, culture and power of adaptability making her acceptable to all classes, and opening doors to service which have never closed. She has filled positions of prominence in unions from local to National and lectured and organized from the Atlantic to the Pacific. Mrs. Washington has contributed to the press in prose and verse from early girlhood, and has published two volumes of poems, "Échoes of Songs" and "Memory's Casket."

Miss Frances J. Griffin, of Montgomery, Alabama, is the daughter of a wealthy planter whose reverses in the war made it desirable that this gifted lady, who seems to have inherited her father's talents and character, should become self-supporting. Miss Griffin brings to the white-ribbon work a brilliant mind and twenty-seven years' drill as a school teacher. She has wit as well as wisdom and a happy faculty of making friends. As National Organizer she has done earnest work in her native state and in Texas, and has won an enviable reputation as a speaker.

Mrs. Mary Bynon Reese, of Chautauqua, Washington, received her baptism for temperance in the great Ohio uprising of 1873-74. She was elected crusade president of the Alliance (Ohio) League, led the first band to the saloons and presided in all the work of the memorable six weeks and for the three succeeding years. She was arrested and imprisoned with thirty-three others in Pittsburg, Pennsylvania, for crusading. Mrs. Reese was one of four ladies who organized Ohio for the constitutional amendment campaign, in which she took an active part; has served the W. C. T. U. as National superintendent for department of Narcotics; has been twice commissioned as World's Missionary to Japan, and for years National Organizer.

Mrs. Emily Pitt Stevens, of San Francisco, California, is the wife of a leading business man in that city, well-to-do in this world's goods, and can give her time without fee or reward, to the work. She has been closely identified with the philanthropies of the western coast and her name is a synonym for good works. She is in private life a model wife and hostess, and in the lecture field her charm of delivery which "thrills from the lips to the heart" has made her one of the foremost speakers of California.

Mrs. Ellen H. Dayton Blair, was one of the crusaders in Pennsylvania. She has been a National Organizer since 1883, and in 1884 began chalk-talking while state superintendent of L. T. L's in Wisconsin. She has given seven hundred illustrated lectures, visiting nearly every state and territory, as well as Canada, and has sent out many hundred sets of her "Outline Charts." As state superintendent of Demorest Medal Contests in Nebraska, she held two Diamond Medal Contests during the amendment campaign, thereby gaining many votes for prohibition. Her husband aids and encourages her in all her work, and like herself, cheerfully sacrifices personal comfort for the white-ribbon cause. Mrs. Blair is now devoting her entire time to the field and is working wonders with voice and chalk.

Mrs. Maude L. Greene, Organizer and Chalk-Talker, though of New England parentage has chosen her home among the grandeur of the Rockies, at Manitou, Colorado. Mrs. Greene is especially happy in her methods of work among children, being one of the most successful artists with chalk, pen and voice. She has an innate sense of humor combined with true devotion to principle, and her "talks" are as pointed as her "chalks." She sketches rapidly, using either or both hands at will. Under the ingenious *nom de plume* of "Ivan Inkling," her pen has won for her a place in the hearts of many readers.

Mrs. E. Rorinne Law, of Detroit, Michigan, identified herself with the W. C. T. U. in 1883, and has since been a zealous and successful worker, rising from one official position to another until she has reached that of National Organizer. A woman of unusual executive ability, backed by strong courage and indomitable faith, she always brings things to pass. To a womanly personality is added a clear and sympathetic voice, which she knows well how to employ in forceful argument. A combined humor and pathos makes her a winning platform speaker.

Miss Belle Kearney, is a native of Mississippi, and although the descendant of a long line of conservative ancestors, was born a radical. At eighteen, she wanted to study law, but was deterred. After spending several years in society, she severed the conventionalities that bound her and began teaching. It was then that she was led to consecrate her life to the service of the Master, and in 1889, she was called to the W. C. T. U. work. Three years after receiving her commission as state organizer of the Young Woman's Branch, she was made National Organizer of the W. C. T. U. As a platform speaker Miss Kearney takes a foremost place among our lecturers and organizers. Her gracious personality and impressive eloquence charm her audiences and win many adherents to the cause she represents.

Miss Ida Clothier is one of our ablest speakers among young women. Born and reared in total abstinence principles she had no close personal knowledge of the liquor curse until thrown among young men and women students in the Boston University. It was while pursuing a special course of study there that the "call" came to active service, and her first W. C. T. U. work was done as state superintendent of Young Woman's Work in Massachusetts. Rapidly developing as a public speaker and organizer, her work soon became national, and she has now lectured and organized in forty different states. Miss Clothier is very successful in presenting the white-ribbon cause to young people's church societies and conventions.

Mrs. Henrietta Skelton, Organizer and Lecturer in the German department, was born in Gissen, Germany, where her father was connected with the University. She married a young English student who became superintendent of a Canadian railway, and in Canada the happy years of her married life were spent. Her husband died after a long and painful illness, during which they together watched through the public prints the uprising of the temperance crusade, and when, soon after he had passed away, Mrs. Youmans called the women of Canada to action, the very first to respond was Henrietta Skelton. Through the years of the early history of the W. C. T. U. she wrought in the eastern and middle states, then later in California. Mrs. Skelton has traversed nearly all the states and territories of the Pacific, preaching the gospel of temperance, and is emphatically a campaigner, while her magnetic personality makes her an impressive speaker, and her sincerity wins friends for herself and the cause she advocates.

Mrs. Frances E. W. Harper has been for more than twenty years the Fred Douglass among colored women. She was born in Maryland in 1825, and although her mother was born a slave, Mrs. Harper had no personal experience of slavery. She first entered the lecture field as an advocate for antislavery, and since the abolition of that evil has devoted her life to the uplift of her own people. She has written several books and is an acceptable speaker on temperance and suffrage platforms.

Miss Clara Parrish entered the W. C. T. U., as have so many of our bright young women, from the school-room. Born and reared upon a farm, she began teaching in the country schools at the early age of fifteen, and only a few years later left a lucrative position as teacher of the sciences in the town of Paris, Illinois, for active work in the Y. W. C. T. U. Since then she has become a National Y organizer and lecturer of acknowledged ability. So pleasing is she in address and so conscientious in methods, that she is repeatedly recalled to the same platform and the same audience. No higher praise can be given.

Miss Frances Hazelton Ensign is an only daughter, residing with her parents at Madison, Ohio. She is a graduate of Oberlin College and was a High School teacher until the call came to her to take up temperance work as the Ohio Y secretary. After three years in this position, which she still retains, she was elected one of the National Y organizers and has since traveled extensively in several states, lecturing and organizing. She conducts the "Kindred Societies" page in *Young Women*, and has recently served as private secretary for Mrs. Frances J. Barnes.

Miss Carrie Lee Carter was born in Stoddard County, Missouri, in 1866, the only daughter and youngest child of indulgent parents. After graduation from college she joined the W. C. T. U., and while engaged in teaching, held many offices in local and county unions, finally becoming president of the largest district in Missouri. Since then she has given her entire time to public work. This bright young woman has been for three years a ruling elder in the Cumberland Presbyterian church. She is a charming speaker and inspires enthusiasm for the white-ribbon cause wherever she goes.

Mrs. Emily A. Kenyon is a mother, a teacher, and a chalk-talker, with fingers that can bring out living pictures on the blackboard, and a brain that can adapt the subject to any audience. Her early home was in Bristol, Rhode Island. In 1869, at the age of twenty-four, she married Dr. H. B. Kenyon, and went with him, a few years after, to Townshend, Vermont. Death broke the home circle in 1892, taking the husband from an active, useful life. Her one son remains, the stay and comfort of his mother, who gives of his fine musical talent to help the temperance cause. Mrs. Kenyon has varied gifts, as her works prove. She leads the Loyal Temperance Legion of Vermont; her deep, rich voice is the bass of the White-Ribbon Quartette that cheers all Vermont state conventions; in medal contest work she has been invaluable and her original Bible readings, illustrated by the board, are sermons never to be forgotten.

Mrs. Martha McClellan Brown is one of our noted pioneers. She was educated in Pennsylvania where her scholarship and powers won her literary titles from two great colleges. There, too, for the sake of the Prohibition party, she declined the state superintendency of schools, offered by the greatest political magnate of the commonwealth. She aided in founding the Prohibition party; was one of the projectors of the National movement at Chautauqua in the summer of 1874; copyrighted the first Bible temperance lessons, and was nine years the editor of a secular paper, the first woman in that field. She is a ready speaker on all current topics; a philosophic thinker and pleasing writer. In addition to lecturing, she speaks almost constantly on Sabbaths by invitation of ministers of all denominations. Mrs. Brown is a native of Baltimore, the wife of Rev. W. K. Brown, D. D., and the mother of six sons and daughters—all of them active, talented, Christian workers.

Mrs. Ellen K. Denny, a temperance worker since crusade days, is descended from a long line of reformers, educators and missionaries. Her husband, Colonel Denny, was a soldier in the war of the rebellion and endured twenty-two months of living death in Libby prison. Mrs. Denny was the originator of the department of Jail and Prison work, and its first superintendent. She has lectured throughout the United States, and is especially successful in the Evangelistic line. Her original manner of reading the Bible and her interpretation of it makes the good old book unusually fascinating to all her hearers.

Mrs. W. Ella B. Gleason, Organizer and Lecturer, is a native of Massachusetts. She commenced speaking in public at nine years of age; graduated from the Eliot High School and taught in the schools of Boston. Marrying early in life, her attention was given to the cares of a family for some years. She has served the W. C. T. U., first as local president, then as county superintendent of Narcotics, state superintendent, and now as National lecturer. In 1892 she was licensed to preach by the Baptist church.

Mrs. Emor L. Calkins was born in Ashford, Cattaraugus County, New York, in 1855; was educated at Griffiths Institute, Springville, New York, and began at sixteen to teach alternate years, to defray the expense of education. She was married to Earle H. Calkins in 1876. In 1881, with their two daughters, they removed to South Bend, Indiana, where for several years she taught elocution. Uniting with the W. C. T. U. she was at once drawn into active service, serving that state as state organizer, superintendent of Schools of Methods and vice-president, and the National as organizer.

Miss Lillian Wood, is a native of Illinois, and of Scotch and English descent. Rev. M. A. Gault, of the National Reform Association, writes: "While lecturing in Missouri, I have many times crossed her track, and have found few workers who have left as lasting imprints upon the hearts of their hearers. She has risen rapidly to be one of the most winning and impressive speakers and workers." Besides that of National organizer and lecturer, Miss Wood holds the position of vice-president of the Missouri state union.

Mrs. Ella Alexander Boole was born at Van Wert, Ohio, in 1858; was graduated at the University of Wooster in 1878, receiving second honors in a class of thirty-one, twenty-eight of whom were young men, and three years afterwards received the degree of Master of Arts. After teaching five years she was married in 1883 to Rev. W. H. Boole, the "Boanerges of Prohibition," a pulpit and platform orator of national reputation. She was elected corresponding secretary of the New York state W. C. T. U. in 1885; held the position for six years, then declining re-election, was made first vice-president, which position she now holds. Mrs. Boole, with her bright, scintillating mind and forceful manner, has developed into one of our best platform speakers.

Mrs. Emily L. McLaughlin of Boston became identified with the W. C. T. U. in Ohio during crusade days, but began her more active career as a public speaker in 1879 in New England. She belongs to a family of orators, and is sister of Rev. Dr. R. R. Meredith, the famous Sunday-school lesson expositor. She is a magnetic speaker, and to her excellence of Christian character adds culture, ladyhood, and that tact which is also talent. Mrs. McLaughlin is president of the Boston union as well as National organizer and lecturer.

Mrs. Addie Northam Field was reared in Illinois. She was a teacher for several years and developed such efficiency in the management of children, that through the influence of Mrs. Rounds, W. C. T. U. president of Illinois, always on the alert to secure talented workers, she was brought to the front as state superintendent of Juvenile work, which position she filled for four years. In 1890 she was married to Rev. Charles H. Field, a Presbyterian minister. Their home is now in New Hampshire, where, until 1894, Mrs. Field was state superintendent of Juvenile work. She was made National Organizer at the Cleveland Convention, and later, at the request of Lady Henry Somerset and Miss Willard, went to England to aid in establishing the L. T. L. department there.

Mrs. Ada Wallace Unrub was born in Indiana in 1853. Of Scotch ancestry she inherits their grit and persistency. The daughter of an early and ardent abolitionist and her character formed in the days of antislavery agitation, she is naturally an enthusiastic lover of liberty. Consequently she is a prohibitionist and woman suffragist of the most radical type. A temperance worker for more than twenty years, she says that she is enlisted in the white-ribbon army to fight it out on this line if it takes, not only "all summer," but all time.

Two National Organizers whose sketches have failed to reach us are **Mrs. S. C. Harris** of Franklin, Virginia, and **Mrs. Sue V. Tomlinson**, of Charlotte, North Carolina.

EVANGELISTS.

Mrs. S. M. I. Henry is the daughter of a Methodist itinerant whose parish extended in early days from the Alleghanies to the Big Muddy. When quite young she developed remarkable literary talent, and Sarepta M. Irish became known to all intelligent Methodists as a poetical writer for the *Ladies' Repository*. The civil war left Mrs. Henry a soldier's widow with three little children to support and train. Her toil in this was heroic, her brain and pen being all the little ones had to depend on. When crusade days came, Mrs. Henry led the forces of Rockford, Illinois, and developing remarkable powers of public address, was called to the front among white-ribboners. She is an evangelist *par excellence*, and has visited nearly all the states in the Union and many of the cities of Canada in the interests of the W. C. T. U. and gospel temperance. Ill health finally compelled Mrs. Henry to give up continuous active work, and for some years the service she has been most often called upon to render is to " Be still and know that I am God."

Mrs. Anna M. Palmer, of Iowa, widow of a Congregational minister, ranks among the oldest of W. C. T. U. workers, being one of the original crusaders. She early identified herself with the W. C. T. U., and was invited to travel as a state worker. In 1885 she was appointed National Superintendent of the Evangelistic department, holding the position for two years, when she became National Evangelist. Mrs. Palmer is a successful and able exponent of gospel temperance, and wherever she goes meets with the hearty co-operation of pastors and churches, often by invitation occupying their pulpits. She has traveled over the length and breadth of the land the past ten years, averaging one address each day.

Mrs. Mary Sparkes Wheeler, author, poet and preacher, was born in England and when six years of age, came with her parents to America. Her father was a man of rare intelligence and literary ability. She began to write for the press at a very early age ; is author of " Poems for the Fireside " and other works, and is a frequent contributor to periodical literature. She is an eloquent and forcible speaker, and has been eminently successful as an evangelist. Her husband is the Rev. Henry Wheeler, D. D., of the Philadelphia Conference of the M. E. church, and the two are united in heart, life and purpose.

Mrs. Harriet D. Walker, of Providence, Rhode Island, is a Methodist Quaker preacher, and was for years an evangelist in New England. Later on she was for years the capable and faithful secretary of the department of Prison and Police Station work. For the last year or two this loyal white ribboner has given herself almost wholly to pulpit and platform work, in which her devoted spirit, ready sympathies and easy flow of language make her adept.

Mrs. Mollie McGee Snell is one of the many bright Southern women whom the temperance work has brought to the front. She is a Mississippian and when the editorial work of the *Sword and Shield* fell from the dead hands of the young martyr-knight, Rhoderic Dhu Gambrell, Mrs. Snell took it up and successfully carried it on. She has been the cause of a famous warfare in the Southern Presbyterian church. Having drawn around her a large Bible class, among whom were men, she was informed that she must not speak to them standing up, or pray, but that she would be allowed to speak to them sitting. The petty persecutions connected with this were so annoying that Mr. and Mrs. Snell withdrew from membership, all of which caused a stirring up among Southern Presbyterians which must be productive of much good.

Mrs. R. J. Trego, influenced by the culture and piety of a Christian home, consecrated herself in early life to the work of saving humanity. Her first work was among the sick. Then temperance work engaged her attention and in her own meetings she has pinned the badge on thousands of reformed men, and told them of a personal Saviour. As lecturer and evangelist, Mrs. Trego speaks from our leading platforms and pulpits, and hundred of souls have been led to Christ through her efforts.

Mrs. Mary J. Weaver, of Batavia, New York, who is state superintendent of Evangelistic work, as well as one of our National Evangelists, is a minister of the Orthodox Friends church. Soon after the death of her husband, twenty-eight years ago, she engaged in gospel temperance work, confining her efforts, until her children were grown, to a field near her home. In recent years she has traveled extensively and thousands have been won to Christ and to our cause through her instrumentality. Last year her state reported two thousand two hundred conversions as the result of the evangelistic work of the W. C. T. U.

Mrs. Elizabeth M. Haughton is an Ohio woman, was educated in the Friends Academy and Earlham College, Indiana ; was married in 1870 to Dr. Richard E. Haughton ; and in 1887 removed to Texas, her present home. She was actively engaged in the crusade, and during succeeding years has conducted . revival services, organized unions, worked in church and Sunday-school and discharged the varied duties of wife and mother. Mrs. Haughton was called to preach when but a girl, and the W. C. T. U. opened up a broad field for her usefulness. Her sweet face, clear tones, and eloquent words are a benediction to those who hear her.

Mrs. Charlotte Comstock Gray was at fourteen years of age an earnest Methodist and a pronounced temperance character. Married in 1872, to a wealthy merchant in Albany, N. Y., she became connected with the charities of that city. She is best known to the W. C. T. U. as president of Albany Union ; superintendent of Sunday-school work in New York state ; delegate to many State and National meetings ; and graduate at Denver as evangelist and deaconess. Alone in the world, and suddenly made homeless by New York state law, Mrs. Gray is now at the University of Chicago, where by Old Testament study and contact with the young life of a " Girls' Dormitory," she is bravely overcoming trouble and fitting herself for larger work.

Miss Cassie L. Smith, born in a Christian home, blessed with Christian teaching, and taught of God in childhood, has been led by His hand all along the way. She spent her early womanhood in school teaching and in music teaching, in 1864 received the pentecostal baptism, and soon afterwards the divine call to the work of an evangelist. She entered upon this ministry with Lois L. Smith, and since the heavenly promotion of her comrade in 1893, she has continued her mission, in connection with churches and the W. C. T. U., as a joyful messenger of the King.

Rev. Frances E. Townsley was born in Albany, New York. Her childhood was spent in Massachusetts, her girlhood in Illinois. She became a Christian at sixteen years of age, and after college days at Wheaton and a few terms of teaching, a call to preach came to her— clear, positive, undoubted. She was licensed to preach by the Shelburne Falls (Massachusetts) Baptist church, in 1874. As an evangelist she has

MARGARET A. SUDDUTH.

traveled in New England, New York and the western States, and in 1885 was ordained pastor of the Baptist church at Fairfield, Nebraska. She is especially noted for her keen perceptions, forceful utterance and tender spirit; is gifted in poetry as well as in prose, and her Bible expositions reveal a deep spiritual insight. Her present home is Howell, Michigan.

Miss Elisabeth P. Gordon, of Auburndale, Massachusetts, is a sister of Anna Gordon and has the clear, quick mind, the loyal, affectionate nature and the indomitable purpose which characterizes all members of the family. She was for seven years corresponding secretary and general organizer for the Massachusetts W. C. T. U. and resigned her position in order to recuperate her overtaxed strength. After some years of retirement from active service she was made National evangelist. No member of the Massachusetts regiment of the grand army of the W. C. T. U. is more beloved.

Miss Elisabeth Sprague Tobey, is a direct descendant of John and Pricilla Alden who came over in the *Mayflower*. She was born and educated in Boston; was converted at twelve years of age, and united with the Trinitarian Congregational church at thirteen. She was for six years state president of the Massachusetts W. C. T. U. and in 1890 declined a renomination in order to give herself entirely to Evangelistic work. She has wonderful power in the wielding of the sword of the Spirit and goes forth to local unions or to churches as she feels called of the Lord.

Miss Anna Downey, (A. M. S. T. B.) is the daughter of Chas. G. Downey, Professor of Mathematics in Asbury University, Greencastle, Indiana. Her mother was a prominent leader in the crusade in that place and died in the "picket" service. She graduated from Asbury University in 1877; was for four years Professor of Mathematics in Iowa Wesleyan University and teacher of Greek in De Pauw University. Believing herself called of God to the work of the ministry, she entered the evangelistic field in 1885. For nine months was pastor of the M. E. Church at Kewanee, Illinois (a privilege arising from the broken health of the regular pastor); completed the course in De Pauw Theological school in 1893 and received the degree Bachelor of Sacred Theology; in 1893 became state superintendent Evangelistic work in Illinois; in 1894 a National evangelist.

Sketches of the National Evangelists, Mrs. J. K. Barney, Mrs. No-rinne Law, and Mrs. J. F. Willing will be found on other pages.

THE WOMAN'S TEMPERANCE PUBLISHING ASSOCIATION.

For sketch of Mrs. Carse, President of the Woman's Temperance Publishing Association, see page 71.

Miss Margaret A. Sudduth, managing editor of *The Union Signal*, though young in years, is in point of service, the senior editor upon the staff of the Woman's Temperance Publishing Association. She was called in July 1887 to a position for which her high and thorough education, extensive travel abroad, Christian temperance parentage, personal character and prohibition convictions made her pre-eminently fit. She first edited the *Oak and Ivy Leaf*, organ of the Y. W. C. T. U., and soon became associate editor of *The Union Signal* also. In 1892, on her appointment as managing editor of *The Union Signal*, she resigned her connection with the young woman's paper. Her warm heart and generous nature keep her constantly alert for opportunities to aid those struggling against adverse circumstances, and she is never happier than when helping some worthy young person to higher aims and efforts. As a writer she is clear, careful and convincing; as managing editor her judgment is seldom at fault, her plans and ideas are rarely misunderstood, and her executive ability is shown by the accomplishment of a vast amount of work, with the least possible evidence of effort. An advocate of woman's progress in every direction, Miss Sudduth is a rare example of the modest dignity which "the new woman" must take on to win respect and the unquestioned right to live on an equality with her brother in public as well as in private life.

Miss Jennie A. Stewart, editor of *Young Women*, and associate editor of *The Union Signal*, is a notable illustration of the developing power of the Y. W. C. T. U. As a home girl, devoted to her invalid mother and younger brothers and sister, she grew interested in the Y in her city, Toledo, Ohio, and soon became its president. An editorial position in the W. T. P. A. was offered and accepted in 1892, and her ability quickly manifested itself, not only in the production of prose and poetry, but in her conduct of the *Oak and Ivy Leaf* (now *Young Women*) and the management of the children's department in *The Union Signal*. Miss Stewart is of Scotch ancestry but was born in Boston, Massachusetts, and educated in Ohio. She combines the sturdy, substantial qualities of her nationality with the brightest of temperaments and a diversity of talents that cause her to do well and cheerfully any task to which her energies are turned.

Miss Ada M. Melville, is an author as well as one of the well-known editors of the W. T. P. A. Her stories, which have appeared frequently in *The Union Signal* during the past six or seven years, have received wide circulation, being copied in English and Australian papers, as well as in those of the home land. As editor of the *Young Crusader*, the children's temperance paper, and literary editor of *The Union Signal*, she finds ample scope for the exercise of her rare literary talents. Miss Melville is a Canadian by birth, but Minnesota was her later home and place of education. She has been associated with the W. T. P. A. five years, and so versatile is her genius and so ready her assistance that she long ago became one of the "indispensables" on the editorial staff.

Mrs. Clara C. Chapin, editor of Books and Leaflets and one of the associate editors of *The Union Signal*, is of English birth and education, trained in total abstinence principles from early childhood. She was first led into public work during the woman suffrage amendment campaign in Nebraska, which state was her home for fourteen years. Later she joined the white-ribbon forces, serving the W. C. T. U., of that state as district president and organizer. Her chief work, however, has been along the line of Press work. Upon removal to Chicago in 1892, she began contributing to the daily papers and to *The Union Signal*, continuing as editorial writer on the latter until called by the W. T. P. A. to her present position in 1894.

Mrs. Caroline F. Grow, Business Manager of the Woman's Temperance Publishing Association, is a native of Rhode Island. She graduated from Wheaton Female Seminary in Norton, Massachusetts, in 1855, and at the age of nineteen became Associate Principal of the Female Seminary at Stamford, Connecticut. Her married life was spent in Chicago and after her husband's death she received practical business training as executrix of his estate. She has had wide business experience, and under her management the W. T. P. A. has won for itself an enviable reputation in Chicago business circles. But Mrs. Grow is not a business woman alone; she is a woman who in early life heard the call of God and devoted herself to His service. In her are blended to an unusual degree both the cool head and the warm heart, each broadened and deepened through the upward look toward God and the outward look upon humanity.

Miss Ruby T. Gilbert, whom Miss Willard rightly denominate the "stanch and true," must be counted among the many jewels grouped in the setting of the W. T. P. A. Her father was for more than fifty years a Baptist minister well known and loved. Miss Gilbert was born in Western New York, but came to Illinois at an early age, where she taught for several years. More than ten years ago she came to the Woman's Temperance Publishing Association as cashier and bookkeeper and has remained ever since in this responsible and exacting position, proving herself a veritable tower of strength.

BUSINESS OFFICE.

MISS JENNIE A. STEWART.

TEMPERANCE HOSPITAL.

MRS. CAROLINE F. GROW.

MATILDA B. CARSE.

NATIONAL TEMPERANCE HOSPITAL.

The National Temperance Hospital was founded to demonstrate the principle that alcohol is not necessary as a remedial agent; and it is doing its work well. The building is located at No. 1619 Diversey avenue, four blocks from the lake and three from Lincoln Park, has all modern conveniences, and is beautifully furnished. In connection with the Hospital is a training school for nurses, which is doing a grand work in training young women to nurse patients in accordance with the principles of non-alcoholic medication.

Mrs. M. E. Kline, President of the National Temperance Hospital Board, brings to that position many qualifications both as a business woman and an experienced W. C. T. U. worker. Left a childless widow when quite young and having a natural turn for business, she gave her attention to mercantile pursuits. From the very inception of the W. C. T. U. its work engaged her heart and mind, and going to Dakota in its territorial days her work made a deep impress for good upon that commonwealth. Coming to Chicago she identified herself with the cause there. Her strong business sense, her promptness and fertility of resource are no unimportant factors in the success of the Hospital.

Mrs. M. M. Hobbs is Vice-President of the Hospital Board and to her devotion is due much of the success of that institution. She has held responsible positions in the W. C. T. U., local, state and National. To her persistency and faithfulness as chairman of the committee which set on foot the Police Matron work in Chicago is largely due the success of this movement. Mrs. Hobbs is an executive officer of many charitable and educational institutions, and has recently presented to the Deaconess' Home of the Methodist church the Deaconess' Orphanage at Lake Bluff, Illinois. A woman of generous impulses and kindly Christian character, she is highly honored and respected in her various fields of labor.

Mrs. Calista Bigelow, Treasurer of the Hospital is a woman preeminently fitted for this important position, having a "business head on her shoulders" that would have made her fortune had she devoted herself to practical affairs. The institution is to be congratulated upon securing one so gifted and accurate to care for its finances.

THE TEMPERANCE TEMPLE.

Mrs. Matilda B. Carse, President of the Board of Temple Trustees, is known the world over as our Temple builder. A Scotch-Irish ancestry, a Presbyterian training, American environments—these were the factors which entered into the make-up of the character needed to carry the crusade fire into the realm of figures and finance.. Mrs. Carse is a worthy descendant of a family that has always been arrayed on the side of philanthropy and reform, and is withal a typical Chicagoan, having lived in that city almost continually since 1858. Her husband, Thomas Carse, was a railroad manager in Louisville, Kentucky, during the civil war. He died in Paris in 1870, leaving Mrs. Carse with three boys under seven years of age. The youngest of these was in 1874 run over by a wagon driven by a beer-soaked German and instantly killed. His tragic death caused his mother to devote her life to the alleviation of the poor and suffering, especially among children. She has been president of the Chicago Central Union since 1878, started the first stock company composed entirely of women—the Woman's Temperance Publishing Association—and has been its president and financial backer from its inception. In 1885 she began planning for the Temperance Temple, National headquarters of the W. C. T. U., which was completed in 1892 at a cost of $1,200,000. Besides the various charities supported by the Chicago Central W. C. T. U., Mrs. Carse is actively interested in many outside philanthropies, and her name is always eagerly sought by benevolent societies and charitable boards. Personally Mrs. Carse is a woman possessing in large degree what we are wont to call "personal magnetism." Few people, men or women, are able to resist her charm of manner, and the times she does not get what she asks for are few indeed. She has been accused of having a dominant will; but had she been less persistent, insistent and resistant the Temperance Temple would never have taken root on terra-firma. · Miss Willard says of her : "For a woman of faith, fortitude and fervor, with financial genius and motherly tenderness of heart, I do not know where we should find her match."

Miss Sara G. Johnson, the Temple's Financial Secretary, comes from Boston, and since 1892 has devoted herself to the enterprise. Of Scotch ancestry she possesses sturdy resolution and strict honesty, while a pleasing address, executive skill and great faithfulness to duty make her a model secretary, and win for her the love of all who come into business or social relations with her.

THE TEMPLE, CHICAGO.

Great Britain.

Organized 1876.

GENERAL OFFICERS.

LADY HENRY SOMERSET.
President.

The sketch of the President of the British Women's Temperance Association will be found on page 4.

MRS. EVA MC LAREN.
Vice-President.

Mrs. McLaren is also World's Superintendent of Franchise and her sketch will be found on page 19.

MRS. AUKLAND.
Corresponding Secretary.

Mrs. Aukland has long been actively engaged in work for the National British Women's Temperance Association in which she takes the greatest interest. She is president of more than one social society and gives much of her time to presiding at and addressing meetings on various phases of woman's work for temperance. Mrs. Aukland originated a scheme for collecting a thousand guineas for the National funds, and has written numbers of letters for the cause of temperance. During the pledge-signing crusade she sent out over two thousand pledge books and has been successful in getting many signatures.

MRS. PEARSALL SMITH.
Recording Secretary.

This sketch will be found under the heading of "Hannah Whitall Smith" on page 12.

MISS MARY GORHAM.

Treasurer.

Miss Gorham's energy and enthusiasm in the white-ribbon movement is almost unrivaled. Besides being treasurer of the National B. W. T. A. she is also superintendent of the Evangelistic department. She travels incessantly, holding evangelistic missions and meetings in the interest of the work throughout the country. Miss Gorham has organized about eighty gospel missions, necessitating the writing of some thousands of letters. She was also successful in organizing a collecting crusade throughout the Association whereby £1,000 was raised by the Branches for the Industrial Farm Home. It is chiefly through her efforts that two hundred pulpits were opened to temperance women in connection with the great convention of the World's W. C. T. U., 1895.

MISS GERTRUDE HUNT.

Office Secretary.

All the official business connected with the work of the National B. W. T. A. goes through Miss Hunt's hands. The responsibility connected with the office makes considerable demand upon her time and thought; but her knowledge and special ability for the position is acknowledged by her co-workers, and those who understand all that official work entails on the staff at headquarters.

OTHER B. W. T. A. WORKERS.

Miss Helen L. Hood ably fills the important office of Superintendent of Organization. She has a genius for this department of work, and has traveled many miles throughout Great Britain and compassed a vast amount of correspondence in her efforts to organize new branches. She is ambitious to see the map of England in her office covered in every county with the little white-headed pins which denote B. W. T. A. Branches in active work for the white-ribbon cause.

The Hon. Mrs. Bertrand Russell is the General Secretary of the Young Woman's Branch, and has inspired the young British women with faith and enthusiasm in the white-ribbon cause throughout England. Mrs. Russell is the daughter of Mr. and Mrs. Pearsall Smith, and is a graduate of Bryn Mawr College, Philadelphia, U. S. A.

Miss Philips, of Tottenham, Superintendent of the Legal department, is a Quaker lady well known for the keen interest she has always taken in the temperance question, and her courageous and successful efforts to bring about the enforcement of existing laws in relation to the liquor trade. On one occasion she gave information against a publican whom she believed sold intoxicants to a drunken man. For this she was arraigned as a malicious persecutor and spy in the court of Mr. Justice Wills. Miss Philips was her own sole witness and gained a verdict with costs, thus securing victory for the cause of woman and temperance.

Mrs. Bamford Slack, the wife of a leading London solicitor, has the Political department under her care and has shown marked ability in this important office. She brings to her work profound thought and unceasing energy and has already proved herself to be a successful propagandist of temperance principles in politics.

Mrs. Bailbache has done untiring work in the cause of Social Purity and is the superintendent for this department in the National B. W. T. A. Her London Home for Women has under her management attained success.

Mrs. Ormiston Chant, whose eloquent lectures on social and literary subjects have made her famous in England and America, is a member of the National Executive Committee of the B. W. T. A. Mrs. Chant has published a book called "Verona, and Other Poems" and a charming book of "Action Songs" for children, and has also preached from scores of prominent pulpits in both countries. Her devoted energies and effective addresses in the interests of purity in personal life and in public amusements, have done much to help form a better public opinion. In leading the crusade against the license and promenade of the Empire Music Hall in London, Mrs. Chant won a moral victory and vindicated the right of women to be heard on public questions, which affect all, irrespective of class or sex.

Mrs. Ward Poole, Superintendent of the Press and Literature department of the National B. W. T. A., has also filled the office of assistant recording secretary, and occasioually lectures in the interests of white-ribbon work. Mrs. Poole is one of the most genial members of the association and her presence at headquarters helps to make all white-ribbon women welcome.

Miss Florence Balgarnie, who is a member of the National Executive of the B. W. T. A., has been officially connected with the association since the reorganization in 1893, and holds the position of Superintendent for the department of Police Matrons. Her euergetic efforts in this work have resulted in drawing public attention to the question, and securing the promise of the Home Government to establish the office of Police Matron in London Police Courts. She has ably advocated the cause of temperance and woman suffrage on the platform and in the press.

Mrs. Osborn has done admirable work in organizing and successfully carrying on the Lecture Bureau. Besides this important line of work, she has established a Lantern Lecture which is now in much demaud. The lecture gives the rise and progress of the Woman's Temperance Movement accompanied by excellent slides.

Mrs. Amie Hicks, who is the Secretary of the Rope Makers' Union, is an indefatigable white-ribbon worker. She has done much to arouse the interest of women in the cause of woman workers and just wages. She is a forceful and earnest speaker, and through her influence there is a growing good understanding between the temperance aud labor movements in England.

Mrs. Wynford Philipps is one of the leading women in the Woman's Liberal Federation and also one of the most eloquent speakers in England. She is a member of the National Executive Committee of the B. W. T. A. and a strong supporter of woman suffrage.

Miss Annie E. Holdsworth is the talented co-editor with Lady Henry Somerset of the *Woman's Signal.* Her literary ability is remarkable and her reputation growing. She has written several novels aud bids fair to win a name among contemporary novelists.

Mrs. Rossiter Willard, the able and experienced manager of the *Woman's Signal*, is also managing editor of the *Woman's Signal Budget*. Her rare business ability and keen insight, accompanied by an affable manner, have made her not only successful in her department but greatly esteemed by British women.

WHITE RIBBON LEADERS IN SCOTLAND.

The Scottish Christian Union of the National B. W. T. A. has branches extending throughout Scotland. Its work is on the departmental system, and has brought many loyal and capable women to the front rank of workers. Space will not permit mention of all our Scottish comrades but foremost among them is their much loved President,

Mrs. Blackie, who is the wife of the distinguished Theological Professor in Edinburgh and whose work of love for the temperance cause has endeared her to many of her sisters in England as in Scotland. Mrs. Blackie celebrated her golden wedding in May this year, 1895, and received many loyal greetings of love and esteem from her friends.

Miss Lees, of Edinburgh and **Mrs. Millar**, Secretary of the Scottish Christian Union, are leaders in the temperance movement in Scotland and widely known for their devoted labors in the woman's cause. They are members of the National Executive of the B. W. T. A.

The British Women's Temperance Association has the following affiliated interests :

1. The *Woman's Signal*, editor-in-chief, Lady Henry Somerset ; corresponding editor, Miss Frances E. Willard ; assistant editor, Miss Annie E. Holdsworth. Offices 33 and 34 Memorial Hall, Farringdon St., London, E. C.

2. The White Ribbon Publishing Company, Limited, with office at Memorial Hall.

3. The Industrial Farm Home for inebriate women, an enterprise that had its inception on the twentieth anniversary of the Crusade.

4. St. Mary's Training Home for girls, at Reigate.

5. Alpha House, Preventive and Rescue Home, 45 Hanley Road, London, N.

Canada.

Organized 1883.

GENERAL OFFICERS.

MRS. LETITIA YOUMANS.

Honorary President.

The white ribbon standard was first planted on Canadian soil by that heroic pioneer, Mrs. Letitia Youmans, who was first president of the Dominion W. C. T. U. and is still its beloved Honorary President. She was born in West Northumberland County, Ontario, in 1827, and spent her childhood and youth on a Canadian farm, experiencing all the rigors and privations of pioneer life. Her thirst for knowledge was intense and when at the age of sixteen a ladies' school was opened in the town of Coburg, to her great joy she was permitted to enter. The following years were occupied in incessant application to study, and after graduation three years were spent in teaching. In 1850 she married and returned to rural life, finding at this time, however, abundant scope for every natural and acquired talent, in a family of eight motherless children and a neighborhood destitute of educational advantages. When the Crusade swept over the states she longed for something of the kind to reach Canada, though her conservative nature scarcely approved of women singing and praying in the streets and in the saloons. Afterwards, meeting leading crusaders at Chautauqua, she saw they were not obtrusive, uncultured women, as she had supposed, and hearing from their own lips the wonderful stories of answered prayer, returned home full of the sacred fire, to devote heart and brain to the destruction of the destroyer in her native land. For eighteen years she continued an indefatigable worker, well known and loved on both sides of the border, and then was called aside to the sick-room whence she pathetically writes: "As I lie on a bed of suffering my prayer is, wash this darkest blot from our country's flag." At the earnest request of white-ribboners in Canada and the United States, Mrs. Youmans has published a book, "Campaign Echoes," which is at once a most interesting autobiography and a valuable history of the temperance movement in Canada.

MRS. LETITIA YOUMANS.

The sketch of Mrs. Ella F. M. Williams, the "loved and lost" President of the Dominion W. C. T. U., will be found among those of other promoted comrades on another page.

HARRIET T. TODD.

Vice-President.

Mrs. Harriet T. Todd was born of New England parentage in the state of Illinois. Before she was three years old the family returned to New York City, where she lived until her marriage with Wm. H. Todd, M. D., of St. Stephen, New Brunswick. Early in the year 1878 a W. C. T. Union was organized in that town; Mrs. Todd was chosen president, and filled that position for several years. Six times she was elected president of the Maritime W. C. T. U., resigning on account of severe illness. In 1892 she was called to the vice-presidency of the Dominion, and is now serving the Union for the third time in that important capacity.

MISS TILLEY.

Corresponding Secretary.

Miss Tilley, of Toronto, has been for years the corresponding secretary of the Dominion W. C. T. U., and one of its "towers of strength." She is the daughter of the celebrated Sir Leonard Tilley, for many years Governor of New Brunswick and Minister of Finance, and for over forty years the most prominent man in temperance work in Canada.

MRS. A. O. RUTHERFORD.

Recording Secretary.

Mrs. Rutherford, of Toronto, is in point of service one of the oldest of Canadian white-ribboners. She is vice-president of the Ontario W. C. T. U., and has been recording secretary of the Dominion since its organization. The Ontario act of 1887 providing for the teaching of temperance in the schools passed while she was superintendent of the department of Scientific Temperance Instruction. Mrs. Rutherford also organized the work among sailors, and was is superintendent for one year.

MRS. TILTON.

Treasurer.

Mrs. Tilton, of Ottawa, is the wife of a leading representative of the government, and has, from the first visit of Miss Willard to Ottawa in 1881, been a devoted champion of the white-ribbon movement.

PROVINCIAL PRESIDENTS.

Mrs. Edith J. Archibald, of Halifax, presides over the three provinces, Nova Scotia, New Brunswick and Prince Edward Island, which are federated as the Maritime Union. She is the daughter of Sir Edward Archibald, for nearly twenty-six years British Consul-General in New York City; was educated partly in New York and partly in England, and was married in 1874 to T. D. Archibald, of Cape Breton, a distant connection and owner of one of the largest collieries on the island. It was here among the employés that Mrs. Archibald learned the significance of the liquor curse and was led into temperance work. Becoming associated with the W. C. T. U., and her comrades quickly discovering and appreciating her worth and capabilities, she was rapidly pushed to the front. A woman of rare attainments in music, art and literature, Mrs. Archibald devotes all her varied talents to the cause of reform. She was the first leader in those provinces to speak and write for woman suffrage. Mrs. Archibald is the originator of the familiar expression " organized mother love," as applied to the W. C. T. U.

Mrs. May R. Thornley, President of Ontario, is a Canadian by birth, but on her marriage went to the United States where she became a prominent W. C. T. U. worker. Returning to Canada a few years later, she threw herself with enthusiasm into the work there, and as president of the London (Ontario) Union raised the membership in one year from a very small number to one hundred and fifty. As superintendent of Schools of Method she rendered valuable aid to the cause.

Mrs. Elizabeth Middleton, Honorary President of the Quebec Union, was born in Yorkshire, England, 1814. She has taken an active interest in the Provincial Union since its formation in 1883, and was its first president. During her five years term of office the sixteen unions grew into sixty-eight, a result only accomplished by great labor and self-denial on her part. She traveled the length and breadth of the English-speaking settlements in the interests of the work. It was only after a severe illness that she relinquished the more active office, but as honorary president the unions still feel her influence and continue to seek her counsel.

Mrs. Mary E. Sanderson, President of the Province of Quebec, is English by birth, but Canadian by training. Reared under the privations and hardships of a pioneer settlement of Western Ontario, that strength of character which has pervaded all her after life was developed. As the wife of a prominent Congregational minister (recently deceased) Mrs. Sanderson has for many years been engaged in active Christian work in the provinces of Ontario and Quebec. Her first introduction into temperance work was in 1883. She has served as local and county president, and at the convention held in Montreal in 1889 was elected president of the Provincial Union. She has ever since devoted much time and energy to consolidating the work. Mrs. Sanderson makes an excellent presiding officer, believing as she has stated, in "just enough red tape to keep things together."

Mrs. D. E. Ruttan, President of Manitoba, is by birth a Canadian, the daughter of a Methodist Episcopal minister; was educated at the Hamilton Ladies' College and the Normal School at Toronto; was married in 1873, and with her husband went to the prairie province from Ontario in 1879. Mrs. Ruttan has been a W. C. T. U. worker since 1888, when Miss Lilian Phelps organized in Manitou, a town which is now known as a stronghold of temperance. Manitoba was the first province to carry the plebiscite and the W. C. T. U. was no unimportant factor in the making of the prohibition sentiment which brought about that result.

Mrs. C. Spofford, President of the W. C. T. U. of British Columbia, is a native of Nova Scotia, but with her parents removed seven years ago to British Columbia, where she became a teacher. She has been in the W. C. T. U. work from its beginning in the province, occupying various positions; was its first corresponding secretary, its second president (when only twenty-four years of age), president of the Y's and twice

president of the local union of Victoria where she resides ; has been corresponding secretary of the managing board of the W. C. T. U. Refuge
Home ever since its establishment and is a leader in church and Sunday-
school work.   As a presiding officer she excels ; as a speaker she is
clear and concise, engaging in manner, possessing an unusually good
voice.   Mrs. Spofford's marked executive ability specially qualifies
her as a leader, and she seems equally well fitted for any position she
occupies.   This is due to her boundless energy, for she believes that
"what is worth doing at all, is worth doing well."

OTHER CANADIAN WORKERS.

Miss Lilian Phelps, of St. Catharines, Ontario, has achieved an
enviable reputation as a speaker.   She is of New England ancestry ; was
educated in St. Catharine's Collegiate Institute and in the Philadelphia
School of Oratory, taking the degree of B. O.   She was first Secretary
of Ontario W. C. T. U. and has been in active service ever since, her
time now being wholly occupied in the lecture field.   Miss Phelps was
World's Fair Commissioner for the Dominion W. C. T. U.

Miss Barber comes of English parentage.   Owing to an accident
in her ninth year she has always had extremely delicate health, but
seldom has there been a life so full of devoted service for others.   For
three years superintendent of Dominion Evangelistic work, she resigned in order to devote her whole time to the more pressing needs
of Provincial and local work.   As superintendent of Social Purity, hundreds of girls have taken the temperance and purity pledge from her
hands.   Endowed by nature with a manner which melts the most har-
dened, and a voice of rare sympathetic quality, Miss Barber has been
very successful in dealing with that class of unfortunate women often so
hard to influence.

Miss Janet E. Dougall, County President for Hochelaga County,
in which Montreal with its seven W. and three Y unions is situated,
is the daughter of the late John Dougall, who came from Scotland in
1826, and early became a leader in temperance work, editing the *Canada
Temperance Advocate* and lecturing through the country.   In 1846 he
published the *Montreal Witness* and later the *Northern Messenger*.   To

the work of these widely circulated papers for half a century is un-
doubtedly due much of the enlightened temperance sentiment of Canada, as shown in the recent plebiscites. Mr. Dougall founded the *New
York Witness* in 1870 and afterwards *Sabbath Reading*. Almost before school years were over Miss Dougall took up various departments
of editorial work on these and other publications. She has been one of
the leaders of the Quebec organization from the first, was for seven
years president of the Montreal Union before it was divided and has
occupied a number of positions in local, Provincial and Dominion W. C.
T. U. work.

Miss Scott, of Ottawa, editor of *The Woman's Journal*, the white-
ribbon organ of Canada, is a young woman of great enterprise and special journalistic talent. She was first superintendent of Young Woman's
Work in Ontario, and for three years has been superintendent of Literature. She is a clever and witty speaker and writer and a white-ribbon
leader of much influence.

Hawaiian Islands.

Organized 1884.

MRS. M. S. R. WHITNEY.

President.

Mrs. Mary S. Rice Whitney is an American by birth and education.
Her father, Lewis L. Rice, was for many years a prominent antislavery
editor in northern Ohio. She is a graduate of Oberlin College. In
1869 she married Dr. J. M. Whitney, and they went to Honolulu,
Hawaiian Islands, where they have since resided, with the exception
of a few years spent in Cleveland, Ohio. When Mrs. Leavitt organized
her first foreign W. C. T. U. in Honolulu, November, 1884, Mrs. Whitney was unanimously chosen president of the society, a position she
has filled acceptably to the present time. Mrs. Whitney is "given to
hospitality." Situated as Honolulu is in the cross-roads of the Pacific,
she often has opportunity to entertain temperance and missionary
workers on their way to or from Australia and Asia and such are
always sure of a hearty welcome from that isolated but energetic little
community.

Japan.

Organized 1886.

The President of Japan, W. C. T. U., Mrs. Kaji Yajima, is one of those whose sketches are regretfully omitted. We take pleasure, however, in presenting to our readers another white-ribbon leader of the Sunrise land.

Madam Sakurai is well known at American headquarters. She is the daughter of a Japanese nobleman, who during the War of the Restoration fought on the side of the Shogun, and for this reason was deprived of his nobility and estates by the Emperor. Thus suddenly impoverished, the family was compelled to perform manual labor for a living, and it was while serving as a waitress in a restaurant at Tokio that this young daughter by her graceful manners attracted the attention of the naval officer to whom she was afterwards married. Through the influence of her English teacher, Mrs. Sakurai and her husband were both led to Christ, and the young officer leaving his excellent position in the navy, entered the Christian ministry and is now pastor of a leading Presbyterian church in Tokio. Mrs. Sakurai established a school in Japan where young women could obtain an English education under Christian influences, and in this way completely revolutionized the whole system of education for women in that country. She was the delegate from the Japan union to the World's W. C. T. U. Convention in Chicago, and afterwards spent some months in Mr. Moody's Bible Institute in that city. She has recently returned to her native land with the purpose of opening a Woman's Bible Institute, in the interests of which she worked and lectured while in the United States.

China.

Organized 1886.

MRS. M. J. FARNHAM.

President.

Mrs. Mary Jane Farnham was born and educated in England. At the age of twenty she was bereft of both parents in a single day by a cholera epidemic, and went to live with her sister in New York. She was married in 1859 to a Presbyterian minister and went with him as a missionary to Shanghai. Besides sharing her husband's labors and caring

MRS. MARY J. FARNHAM.

for her family, Mrs. Farnham conducted a free day school for poor girls and a large boarding school. A total abstainer from childhood, she was always interested in temperance work, and when Mrs. Leavitt went to Shanghai was rejoiced to welcome her to her home, and later to co-operate with Miss Ackerman, and Mrs. Andrew and Dr. Bushnell in their work in China. With many cares and amid almost insuperable obstacles Mrs. Farnham has pushed the white-ribbon work in the Celestial Empire with the faithfulness and self-sacrifice so characteristic of the missionary spirit.

Miss Ruth Shaffner, first superintendent of the department of Organization for the National W. C. T. U. of China, gathered her enthusiasm for the work from the fire of the crusade. She went to Canton at the close of her college career as pioneer missionary from the church of the United Brethren. She soon became convinced that the strategic point of attack was the schools and through her efforts in conjunction with those of Mrs. Mary H. Hunt, a set of reliable Temperance Physiologies was translated into Chinese. Miss Schaffner represented the Chinese Union at the World's Conventions in Boston and Chicago, urging there the necessity of a W. C. T. U. specialist for Chinese work. She participated in the great Polyglot Petition meeting in Washington with the joy of one who had helped collect those strange signatures that "look like the houses that Jack built." For the past three years she has occupied the position of school-mother for over three hundred girls at the Indian Industrial School, Carlisle, Pennsylvania.

India.

Organized 1887.

MRS. MARY R. PHILLIPS.

President.

Mrs. Mary R. Phillips, of Calcutta, went to India with her missionary husband in 1864. Her first work was among the zenana women, later among the neglected children of the streets, three hundred of whom she gathered into schools under her own superintendency. In April, 1894, upon Mrs. Hauser's resignation, Mrs. Phillips became President of India, and has carried forward the plan of work begun by her predecessor with a remarkable degree of success. New methods adopted under her leadership promise to bring this newly organized auxiliary of the World's W. C. T. U. to the front among national organizations. One who knows Mrs. Phillips well writes of her: "She seems to know how to bring to the front the best that is in one. Her public addresses are helpful and inspiring and so beautifully simple that she wins the hearts of all listeners." Mr. Phillips is in hearty sympathy with his wife's work, and as secretary of Sunday-school work in India is an immense help in forwarding the white-ribbon cause.

RAMABAI.

World's W. C. T. U. Lecturer.

This rare character is recognized in her own country as the greatest Hindu woman that has lived. She is the daughter of a Marathi priest and can trace her Brahmin ancestry a thousand years. Her father, having resolved, in defiance of the laws of custom and conventionality, to educate his wife, retired to a forest home to carry out his ideas without molestation. There in 1858 Ramabai was born, and there, in entire seclusion, was educated by her parents. Orphaned before she was sixteen she traveled several years with her brother, a noble young man, who sympathized with her in her determination to devote herself to the elevation of her countrywomen. The degree of Sarasvati was conferred upon her by the University of Calcutta, she being the first woman in the empire to be thus honored.

Ramabai married a Bengalese gentleman, a lawyer, whom she freely chose—this being an instance almost without precedent. He died within two years, leaving her at twenty-four with an eight-months baby. She went to England, was made professor of Sanskrit in Cheltenham College, and in 1886 came to America to see her cousin graduate from the Woman's Medical College of Philadelphia and to study our educational methods.

Ramabai lectured in our principal cities and wrote a book, "The High Caste Hindu Woman," during her stay in this country, raising sufficient money to open a school for child-widows in India, which is rapidly increasing in power for good. The Pundita is a thorough-going white-ribboner and is lecturer for the World's W. C. T. U. in India. Miss Willard says of her: "Her gentleness exceeds any other manifestation of that exquisite quality that I have yet seen; this tenderness, all-embracing as to the human race, extends with her to every sentient creature."

PUNDITA RAMABAI.

Cape Colony.

Organized 1887.

MISS THERESA CAMPBELL.

President.

Miss Campbell is a native of New York, having first worked for Africa as a missionary in Egypt, and since as teacher in the Young Ladies' Seminary at Wellington, Cape Colony. She was the representative of South Africa to the World's Convention in Boston, and was Colonial Vice-President until the resignation of Miss Pride in 1893 when she was elected in her place. Miss Campbell is editor of *The White Ribbon for South Africa*, giving not only her time, but a large portion of her income to the printing and circulation of this paper and other temperance literature.

France.

Organized 1888.

MISS DE BROEN.

President.

Miss De Broen, the white-ribbon standard bearer in France, is best known through her work in connection with the Bellevue Mission, of which she is founder. After the Franco-German war of 1870 Miss De Broen began her work among the Communists. She first established sewing classes, and from this nucleus arose the present large and influential Bellevue Mission. The medical mission established by her was for a long time the only one on the continent of Europe. Full of mental resource though she is, it is no easy task to maintain this enterprise with its physicians, evangelists, women to visit and teach, the orphanage of girls, the sewing classes, temperance meetings, Sunday-school, night schools for adults and the children's day school, but to the superintendence of this immense work Miss De Broen devotes her life. In the words of a French Society which presented her with their silver medal, "The moment she chose for the establishment of this work in the Bellevue district was when the heart of France lay bleeding; her aim being to draw the people out of their profound despair by the light of the gospel. And she has succeeded!"

Natal.

Organized 1889.

MRS. MARY FERNIE.

President.

Mrs. Mary Fernie, of Sydenham, is the Colonial President, elected in 1894. She is of English birth, but has spent many years in Natal, her husband being the pastor of the Congregational church at Sydenham. Mrs. Fernie is in the prime of life and has brought a large degree of energy and consecration into her office, deeming no work too difficult if it will advance the influence and show forth the helpfulness of the organization.

Spain.

Organized 1891.

MRS. ALICE GORDON GULICK.

President.

Mrs. Gulick is the sister of Anna and Bessie Gordon and shares with them the philanthropic temperament. She is a graduate with honor of Mt. Holyoke College, where she afterwards taught; has been for twenty years the wife of the Rev. Wm. Gulick of the famous missionary family of that name, and has shared his work in Spain under the auspices of the American Board. They conduct a school for girls in San Sebastian — the only evangelical school for girls in Spain — and have among the pupils a Y organization and an L. T. L.

South African Republic.

Organized 1891.

MRS. MARY F. GRAY.

President.

Mrs. Gray was the first president of the W. C. T. U. of Harrismith, Orange Free State, her husband being pastor of the Presbyterian church. She is the daughter of Rev. Wm. Tyler, of St. Johnsbury, Vermont, who was many years missionary among the Zulus. It was through the gentle persuasiveness of Mrs. Gray's influence that Pretoria and Johannes-

burg, the chief gold mining centers in South Africa, have each a W. C.
T. U. and a Y branch, and that juvenile temperance work is so flourish-
ing in those towns.

OTHER SOUTH AFRICAN WORKERS.

Mrs. Laura Bridgeman, American Mission Station, Natal, was
the first W. C. T. U. president of an auxiliary society in South Africa,
having been appointed by Mrs. Leavitt to that office, and called the first
W. C. T. U. Convention ever held in South Africa, in June, 1889. Mrs.
Bridgeman now edits two columns of W. C. T. U. notes weekly for a
leading Natal paper. We have no woman in any country with more of
the true Christian temperance spirit.

Mrs. Howard Sprigg was first president of the Transkie, "a local
union as large as Ireland." She traveled in 1893 one thousand miles
in her own private conveyance in the interest of this work. In 1894 her
husband was made chief magistrate of Pondoland, and she removed
farther east, becoming president of Pondoland where her power among
soldiers, natives and all classes of humanity is beyond computing. Her
sister, Miss Bate, of Blytheswood, is president of the Transkie.

Mrs. Anna James, of Harrismith, though doing the quiet work of
the president of a local union, has spent hundreds of dollars in sowing
the Orange Free State with W. C. T. U. literature. It is through her
influence that Harrismith has already contributed two hundred dollars
to the Temperance Temple in Chicago. Her loyalty and generosity
and that of her late husband toward schemes for "home protection"
are spoken of throughout the eastern part of South Africa.

Mrs. Murray, wife of the Rev. Andrew Murray, is superintendent
of the department for Purity, and has addressed personally or by letter
every minister in South Africa on this theme within the past two years,
besides writing constantly to leaders in England and America to secure
literature and the best method of prosecuting the work she has so
bravely undertaken, viz., that of securing the repeal of the "C. D.
Acts."

Australasia.

Organized 1891.

MRS. E. W. NICHOLS.

President.

Mrs. Elizabeth Webb-Nichols, who presides over the federated unions of Australasia, was born in Adelaide, in 1850, and is descended on both sides from religious and literary families. At the age of fifteen she entered the ranks of Christian service by joining the Wesleyan Methodist church. She was married in 1870 to Mr. A. R. Nichols, a business man, a Sunday-school worker, and a total abstainer, who is in entire sympathy with the methods of the white-ribbon organization. Mrs. Nichols first became a total abstainer in 1875, signing the pledge for the sake of example in the Sunday-school. She first came into touch with the W. C. T. U. during Mrs. Leavitt's meetings in Adelaide, in 1886, when she was made president of the Adelaide union. In 1889, at the first Colonial convention she was elected Colonial President; in 1894, to the very honorable and onerous position of Australasian President, to succeed Miss Ackerman. Mrs. Nichols is a woman of both business and literary ability, of striking personality and a face which inspires love and confidence. Her genial disposition, quick sense of humor and thorough knowledge of parliamentary usage makes her an ideal president.

Norway.

Organized 1892.

COUNTESS WEDEL-JARLSBERG.

President.

No cause could desire an abler leader than has Norway in Ida Countess Wedel-Jarlsberg. Of high birth and noble family, of fine education and large experience, it is a wide outlook that she can take over the ills and sufferings of sinning humanity. While she is respected and honored in all circles, from the court downwards, she is one who esteems most highly her service for the King of kings and her connection with the court of heaven. No one could commend the white-ribbon cause more intelligently or effectively to her countrymen than the Countess Wedel, while in personal appearance, eloquence and tact she may well stand side by side with the foremost temperance platform leaders of the world.

Mexico.

Organized 1894.

MRS. B. B. BLACHLY.

President.

Mrs. Blachly is the daughter of a Congregational minister, and was born in Prairie City, Illinois, the ninth child in a family of thirteen. Her childhood's ambition was to become a teacher. At the age of eighteen she left home and with the help of a brother and by working during vacations and after school hours, she managed to complete her education. During these years she became interested in reform work, especially in temperance. She taught school for nine years and in 1893 married Mr. Blachly, who had been for four years in the employ of the American Bible Society in Mexico. Mrs. Blachly soon discovered the great need of temperance work in her new home, and has been earnest in her efforts to arouse people to the fearful ravages of the rum traffic in Mexico. In 1894 she was appointed president of the W. C. T. U. of that Republic auxiliary to the World's Union.

We regret very much that the limited time given for the compilation of this book has made it impossible to procure sketches of the presidents of all auxiliaries of the World's W. C. T. U. We hope in the near future to supply the missing links in the white-ribbon chain which encircles the globe. The order followed in the partial list given is that of the last World's Leaflet.

PIONEERS.

MOTHER THOMPSON.

That "saint in Israel," Mrs. Elizabeth J. Thompson, is known and loved by white-ribboners around the world as the Crusade Mother. She is of Virginian ancestry, the only daughter of a governor of Ohio and wife of a distinguished judge, and was surrounded in her earliest years by Christian influences whose voices were never forgotten through the long life now well past the threescore and ten of sacred writ. As daughter, wife, mother, grandmother, seeking no great things in life, Mother Thompson was prepared by the great Leader himself as a leader for a supreme hour. It came about that being kept away from Dio Lewis' meeting on the historic 23rd of December, 1873, by home cares, this faithful mother was all unprepared for the call that came to her from that great gathering. There is no small significance in the fact that it was her son and daughter who urged the retiring little mother forward in the path prepared for her, and that it is because of a daughter's love and knowledge of the Word that hundreds of thousands of women have written upon their hearts the Crusade Psalm. And now that mother's hair is white, and the feet that led the timid band of women from the house of prayer, to the doors across whose threshold passed sin and crime, go very softly on the way of life. She has had love and praise and publicity for twenty years, yet her comings in and her goings out are marked by a beautiful quietude and unconsciousness of self. Many are the "daughters" who have risen up and many more are they who shall rise up around the world to "call her blessed."

MOTHER STEWART.

Mrs. Eliza D. Stewart, of Springfield, Ohio, is a woman of indomitable purpose, dauntless courage, and withal most pleasing personality. Born a leader, she has led the right in many a triumphal march against wrong. She began, publicly, her warfare against rum in 1858. Seeing that public sentiment was asleep to the evils of intemperance, she made it her mission to arouse the slumbering forces with her clarion cry, and the echo of that cry is still heard around the world. She was the first woman to go into the civil courts and plead the case of a drunkard's wife, and was the prime mover of a great tidal wave of temperance in

MOTHER THOMPSON.

MOTHER STEWART.

her own city, which was the forerunner of the crusade. She formed the first union ever organized, and also introduced the W. C. T. U. work into Great Britain, the British Women's Temperance Association being a result of her efforts. Her histories, "Memories of the Crusade," and the "Crusader in Great Britain," must be read to be rightly appreciated. One, writing of her, says : "To form any idea of her physical labor and travels, you must read her books ; to judge her great, loving, motherly heart, you must come in touch with results as felt by those she has lifted ; to know the length, breadth and depth of her good works, you must make sure of heaven and listen when the books are opened."

ABBY F. LEAVITT.

Mrs. Abby Fisher Leavitt was one of the prominent figures of the Ohio crusade. Maine was her birthplace and early home, and at the age of nineteen she graduated from the high school of Bangor. She went South as a teacher, became principal of a grammar school in Evansville, Indiana, and there married Samuel K. Leavitt, a lawyer, who was later ordained a Baptist minister. Mrs. Leavitt was leader of the "Praying Band" in Cincinnati, and while engaged in crusade work was, with forty-two others, arrested and taken to jail. When the band was reorganized into the Woman's Christian Temperance Union she was chosen president. She was for years treasurer of the National Union and her appeals for help, at once so witty and convincing, were among the memories of the convention. Among the ablest and most constant friends of our National paper Mrs. Leavitt should ever be remembered. For two years a member of its publishing committee, she invested much time, thought and prayer in its behalf.

ANNIE WITTENMYER.

Mrs. Wittenmyer was first President of the National Woman's Christian Temperance Union, and served in that capacity for five years. She was one of the founders of *Our Union* the first official organ, which was afterwards consolidated with *The Signal* and became *The Union Signal*. She wrote "The History of the Woman's Temperance Crusade," a book of eight hundred pages giving a history of that wonderful movement. Mrs. Wittenmyer has been connected editorially for the last twenty years with magazines and leading newspapers, is the author of a number of books, and her Christian hymns have been sung around the world. Her book, "Under the Guns" gives thrilling experiences of the civil war, during which, she was sanitary agent for the state of Iowa, and later in the service of the Christian commission. She has also been president of the Woman's Relief Corps. Mrs. Wittenmyer was born in Ohio but her early home was Kentucky; she is descended from an old and influential family; is a Daughter of the Revolution, and the founder of a number of benevolent institutions.

EMILY HUNTINGDON MILLER.

Mrs. Emily Huntingdon Miller, now Dean of the Woman's College in the Northwestern University at Evanston, Illinois, was secretary of the Chautauqua meeting which sent out the "call" for the first National convention. She was born in Brooklyn, New York, in 1833; educated at Oberlin College; married in 1859 to Mr. John E. Miller, at first professor of Ancient Languages, afterwards a publisher and prominent Sunday-school worker, and whose death some years ago removed one of the truest friends of the W. C. T. U. Whoever has read Mrs. Miller's stories —and what child has not?—knows that Mrs. Miller is a stanch temperance woman. The chief feature of *The Little Corporal*, one of the most popular of children's papers ever published, was a series of stories from Mrs. Miller's pen. She contributes both prose and poetry to many papers and magazines and has written several juvenile books, besides giving lectures on temperance, missionary and educational subjects. On one thing she particularly prides herself, viz., her ability to make bread and darn stockings with any woman living.

JENNIE FOWLER WILLING.

Mrs. Willing was born in Burford, Canada West, in 1834. When she was eight years old her parents removed to Illinois and she grew up in the surroundings of country life and with such scanty schooling as the Prairie state could furnish in that early day. She married at nineteen, Rev. Dr. W. C. Willing, a knight of the new chivalry, who delighted in and encouraged his wife's literary aspirations, and until his death in 1895, was a warm friend of the W. C. T. U. Later on we find Mrs. Willing Professor of English Language and Literature in Illinois Wesleyan University, and preparing essays, serials, sermons and orations. When the crusade sounded its muster-drum Mrs. Willing was among the first to enlist. She presided at the preliminary meeting at Chautauqua in 1874, issued the call for the first W. C. T. U. convention and presided over it at Cleveland the same year. She was first editor of our National paper and was for years state president of Illinois. In 1873 she was licensed as local preacher in the M. E. church and her revival meetings are scenes of especial· power. She is a volumiuous writer aud in car or steamer is always busy with book or pencil. Mrs. Willing is a sister of Bishop Fowler of the M. E. church. She possesses rare culture of manner and of utterance, a steady purpose and consecrated heart, and like all strong souls has for her motto "*plus ultra* "— more beyond.

MARY B. INGHAM.

Mrs. Mary B. Ingham, an Ohio woman born and bred, is the child of a pioneer Methodist preacher ; her mother a noble woman giv" ing to her children a heritage of industry, thrift and executive ability. Educated in four languages, Mrs. Ingham early wrote for publication. In 1870 she became a leader in the Woman's Foreign Missionary Society and in 1874 planned and led the crusade in her home city, Cleveland, Ohio, and later on became one of the founders of the W. C. T. U. At the age of sixty, youthful aud vigorous, she is elected general secretary of Young People's work in the Woman's Home Missionary Society.

MRS. MARGARET E. PARKER.

Mrs. Parker, of Dundee, Scotland, was the first woman across the sea to catch the inspiratiou of the crusade, and when the British Women's Temperance Association was organized in 1876 became its first president. Born a conservative and reared in all the prejudices of aristocratic birth she overleaped these barriers, and in the face of opposition which would have crushed a soul less brave, became a philanthropist and reformer. "Au orthodox of the orthodox," she worked for woman suffrage side by side with the party of John Stuart Mill ; a wife, mother and housekeeper of the New England school, she addressed the British Social Science Congress on the question of capital and labor ; a modest, soft-voiced woman from the home-hearth and the cradle-side, she marshaled "the bonnets of bonny Duudee," leading a processiou of sixty of her townswomen to the headquarters of the magistrate where they presented a no-license petition with nine thousand names of women. Twice since the crusade Mrs. Parker has visited our country, and a charming little book, "Six Happy Weeks Among the Americans," records her impressions of the land she had so long desired to see.

MARY B. WILLARD.

Mrs. Mary Bannister Willard is the daughter of Rev. Dr. Henry Bannister, for many years principal of Cazenovia Seminary, New York, and later professor of Hebrew in Garrett Biblical Institute in the North-western University at Evanston, in which latter institution Mary took the classical course. She was married to Oliver A. Willard, brother of "our Frances," and until his death, sixteen years later, found in her home and children, labors and cares which to her loyal heart meant the putting aside of the "career" to which by nature and training she was exceptionally called. As editor of *The Signal*, afterwards *The Union Signal*, Mrs. Willard abundantly demonstrated her ability as a journalist; she also came to the front as one of Illinois' foremost speakers and organizers. In 1885 she went to Berlin, Germany, for the further education of her daughters and seeing the need of such an institution, remained there to establish the "American Home School for Girls." Miss Willard says of her: "She is a woman of abounding spirituality, whose intuitions of Christ, conscience and immortality, supplemented by life-long Bible study, anchor her firmly in a broad, deep, living faith which no outward circumstance of bereavement or disaster has in the least degree disturbed."

SARAH K. BOLTON.

The name of Sarah K. Bolton, author and poet, is national and world-wide. She has by voice and pen stood by our great movement from the first, has written a history of the crusade, and set forth our work in most influential quarters on both sides of the sea. She is a woman of special gifts and culture as a journalist, and as a member of the editorial staff of the Boston *Congregationalist* did us excellent service. As assistant secretary of the National W. C. T. U. in its early days, she kept articles, paragraphs and enlightening excerpts before the public which served to set our new methods before the public. In her speech before the Cleveland Convention in 1894, Mrs. Bolton said, "The grand thing about our work is that the young people are coming on to take our places. I am glad to have my only boy proud of his mother as a crusader."

MARGARET E. WINSLOW.

Miss Margaret Winslow is one of the long list of white-ribbon notables who dates her "ordination" from the crusade. She was one of the early editors of *Our Union;* is a contributor to various leading magazines and religious papers and the author of several story books. It was a burst of inspiration from Miss Winslow which at the Chicago convention determined the W. C. T. U. to wear the white ribbon badge rather than the red-white-and-blue which was strongly urged by many. "White," suggested Miss Winslow, "is the emblem of both purity and the resultant of all the other virtues, and," quoting Keble's words,

"As every varied hue makes white,
So every grace is love."

CRUSADE CHURCH.

PROMOTED.

Ah! comrades we stand in the silence
    Homesick for a day,
But how can our anguish be bitter?
    We follow that way.
Let us lift up our hearts, our beloved,
    Love on as of yore;
Who knows but in stress of the battle
    They haste to the fore?
"Then onward, ye brave," to the duty,
Not far, with the King in His beauty,
    We greet them once more.

                   —MARY T. LATHRAP.

MARGARET BRIGHT LUCAS.

The veteran reformer, Mrs. Margaret Bright Lucas, passed through the "portal we call death," to her heavenly home, on February 4, 1890, at the age of 71. She was first president of the World's W. C. T. U. and preceded Lady Henry Somerset as president of the British Women's Temperance Association. Of Quaker ancestry and training, the sister of John Bright, the noted British commoner, with wealth, position and an honored name, Mrs. Lucas brought to our ranks gifts many and rare. She was president of the Bloomsbury branch of the Women's Liberal Association, and lost no opportunity in all her public addresses of emphasizing the fact that temperance legislation, to be successful, requires woman's vote, and as far back as 1883, in her annual address before the B. W. T. A., she urged her co-workers to study this question with regard to its bearing upon their work. In 1886 Mrs. Lucas paid her second visit to America as a delegate to the National W. C. T. U. in Minneapolis, at which time she received a most enthusiastic reception, and Miss Willard, in her address, turning to her British sister and clasping her hand, said, "For the first time in history the imperial mother and the dauntless daughter of the Anglo-Saxon race clasp hands in a union never to be broken."

(98)

MARGARET BRIGHT LUCAS.

MISS JULIA A. AMES.

SARAH J. C. DOWNS.

For ten years Mrs. Downs, our "Andrew Jackson," led the women of New Jersey. When she became president she found twenty-four unions—a thousand members. When she laid down her work, there were two hundred and twenty unions and eight thousand white-ribbon women in New Jersey. The widow of a Methodist minister, she came to the work of the Woman's Christian Temperance Union as she was nearing her sixtieth year. With psalms of praise and victory, she went on like a conqueror to her place with the glorified, and her last words were, "The liquor traffic will be outlawed; blessed is he who helps"—prophetic of the future and characteristic of her mind and heart. "If Mrs. Downs had lived fifty years later," said Miss Willard, "she would have become Governor of New Jersey, or a Bishop in the Methodist Episcopal church, for in her were united the deepest mother-heart and the bravest brotherly brain."

JULIA A. AMES.

Miss Julia A. Ames was almost the first young woman of National fame in the white-ribbon ranks to leave her earthly home for the heavenly. Born near Streator, Illinois, in 1860, she lived her short, beautiful life on the prairies of her native state and in its chief city — Chicago. She died on December 12, 1891, in Boston, Massachusetts, whither she had gone a month previous to attend the National and World's W. C. T. U. Convention. Press work was her specialty in the temperance field. This she began in a modest way in Chicago, soliciting from the daily papers a half column's space each week. So successful was her local work, that she was made National superintendent of the Press department, and associate editor on *The Union Signal* in 1886. This latter position she held at the time of her death, having risen, however, by her unusual journalistic talent, as well as by her unfailing judgment and sweet courtesy of manner to co-equal editorship with Miss Mary Allen West. In 1889 Miss Ames went to England as fraternal delegate to the British Women's Temperance Association, where her address on press work and her own charming personality made a most favorable impression upon her English sisters, and was one means to the establishment of the Press department in the British Association. In the thought of many Miss Ames is the beautiful but now unseen link between our two beloved leaders, for Lady Henry says: "Her glowing words of admiration and the deep love with which she spoke of her great leader, only increased my earnest desire to know Miss Willard." One of the pathetic features of this book is that Miss Ames was its editor, when first brought out four years ago in another form, and only a few weeks before her lamented death.

JENNIE CASSEDAY.

Our "white-ribbon saint," the founder and first superintendent of Flower Mission work, went home on February 8, 1893, after thirty years spent on a bed of pain. She was born in Louisville, Ky., in 1840, one of a family noted for its gifts and graces of mind. Her girlhood was passed amid the bright surroundings of a wealthy Christian home. Just as Miss Casseday was stepping across the threshold of womanhood she was thrown from a carriage, and the spinal injury which resulted made her a physical invalid and an intense sufferer for life. It was her own love of flowers in the sick-room which first suggested the Flower Mission, and when Miss Willard went to Louisville in 1881, she gained Miss Casseday's consent to become superintendent of this work for the W. C. T. U. From that time to the day of her death she directed from her sick-bed world-wide plans for this beautiful philanthropy, personally conducting an immense correspondence in its interests. Besides her work in the Flower Mission, Miss Casseday was the founder of the Jennie Casseday Infirmary, and the Louisville Training School for Nurses. She also established "Rest Cottage," a summer home for working girls. "Jennie Casseday was," say Kentuckians, "the best-loved woman in her state." She erected monuments more enduring than marble and brass, and generations yet unborn will call her blessed.

MADAM WILLARD.

The story of the beautiful life of our "Saint Courageous" has been told by the pen of a mighty love and the world to-day unites to do homage to Mary T. Hill Willard as "A Great Mother." Born in Vermont, she early removed to Western New York, and from there, in married life, to Oberlin, Ohio, and later, to Janesville, Wisconsin. Her character was a marked blending of the strength and rugged grandeur of New England's granite hills, with the breadth and wind-swept freedom of the Western prairies. She was a successful school-teacher until her marriage with Josiah F. Willard, and into the training of her children she carried the same enthusiasm and the same willingness to adapt

MADAM WILLARD.

MARY ALLEN WEST.

MARY A. WOODBRIDGE.

means to the end which had characterized her as a teacher. No cast-iron methods for child-culture were embraced by her. Her conception of the value of her own individuality made her guard as equally sacred the individuality of her children. Long before Froebel became a household name her wise head and wiser heart had adopted many of his methods. "Let a girl grow as a tree grows," was the motto which, lived out in that prairie home, and later during Evanston's college days, gave to the world Frances E. Willard.

A close student of current events, a careful reader, an original thinker, one could not be in Madam Willard's presence without recognizing the presence of a great mind. But it was in the realm of soul-life that her greatness was most manifest. There, indeed, she towered above the world into the realm of the infinite. Her calmness and quiet peace were not born of inactivity or indifference—they rather sprang forth from the faith which above, beneath and around all struggles and all trials sees and knows God.

She possessed a quaint humor, a rare power of epigram, a wholesome hearty gladness in life. She believed in God and therefore believed in God's children—humanity. The white-ribbon movement which came to her when she had reached the borderland of old age, came as no new revelation, it was simply the expression of her own thought and purpose. She entered into it, heart and soul, and from that day until "the great sunset," which crowned her life August, 1892, no woman was more truly an incentive and an inspiration to the peaceful hosts the world over. Though "gone before" she leads us still.

MARY ALLEN WEST.

Mary Allen West has been in heaven two years and a half, but she is not forgotten on earth. Her name is to-day a cherished one in thousands of hearts and homes. It is difficult to place special prominence upon any one of her many honorable positions. As a teacher in the college and high school of her native town, Galesburg, Illinois, for twenty years, as superintendent of the public schools of the county (Knox) for nine years, as president of the Illinois W. C. T. U. for five years, as senior editor of *The Union Signal* and National superintendent of Schools of Methods for seven years, and as an active round-the-world missionary in Japan for three months, she rounded up a life of fifty-five years of usefulness and consecration so rare that even those who knew of her daily application to duty and genuine love of service, marvel to this day.

Dying upon foreign soil, December 1, 1892, as the direct result of overwork in organizing and speaking, Miss West left the Christian workers of two nations—America and Japan—in mourning. The Christian Japanese women in many places said : " She is indeed our mother, for by her motherly kindness and suffering our W. C. T. U. was born." Aside from holding the positions named, Miss West was an author and Sunday-school teacher of deserved fame. Her largest and most important book, "Childhood : Its Care and Culture," has met with great favor, for she was, as some one has truly said, "a natural mother." She "mothered" everything; her work and her associates were always her children. "My girls," meaning all the women employés of the Woman's Temperance Publishing Association, was constantly on her lips, even in far-distant Japan, where she was alert to pick up some little treasure for each. And in Sunday-school teaching it was more than once whispered around that "mothers who were not willing to have their daughters go to the ends of the earth as missionaries would better keep them out of Mary Allen West's class ! " And no wonder, for eight young ladies went from that one class in one town to foreign fields of Christian labor. Miss West knew the W. C. T. U. as she knew her Bible and it was her chief delight to teach its methods to others. If she had lived, doubtless, her final specialty would have been her Schools of Method, traveling from town to town and establishing herself as leader with the local officers for her faculty. Self-denial and almost unceasing labor were her main pleasures on earth, and she has left behind her hundreds of friends, who praise her noble life and profit by her love and devotion to humanity and God.

MARY A. WOODBRIDGE.

Mary A. Woodbridge came by rightful inheritance into the possession of her quick intellect, her insatiable love of books and learning, her well-rounded mind and peaceful, gracious dignity. She was born in 1830 in the old town of Nantucket. Her gentle, refined Quaker mother was a sister of Mitchell, the astronomer, whose only daughter Maria became so famous. Her father, Isaac Brayton, was a sea captain and afterwards a member of the Massachusetts legislature. Mary, at the age of seventeen, married Mr. F. W. Woodbridge, a young business man, and for forty-seven years theirs was an ideal home. Mrs. Woodbridge was more than forty years old before that magnificent voice of hers, which contributed so much to her power, had ever been heard in public ; but when the crusade swept her state it was to her as a call from God to new duties. For five years she was president of the Ohio W. C. T. U., leading in the famous amendment campaign, and editing *The Amendment Herald*. In 1877 she was elected assisant recording secretary of the National W. C. T. U., and in 1878 recording secretary. In 1889 she was appointed America's Secretary for the World's W. C. T. U. ; in 1891 elected World's Secratery, and in 1893 was made Corresponding Secretary of the National, thus for eleven months holding a threefold position of responsibility. At the zenith of her powers she left us ; left us without a warning—at her desk one day and the next stricken with death. "I should be perfectly happy," she once said, "to die with the harness on," and that happiness was hers. The most striking elements of Mrs. Woodbridge's character was her unspoiledness and self-effacement in the midst of her honors, the cheerful, dignified brightness and joy of her personal bearing, and the deep piety which was the bed-rock of her nature.

MARY TORRENS LATHRAP.

On January 3, 1895, Mary T. Lathrap left us to join the heavenly host. She was known as the "Daniel Webster" among white-ribboners and as our "peerlesss prohibition pleader"—invincible in argument, eloquent in oratory, masterful in all her ways, yet "touched into love and sympathy as readily as she could be roused into heroic action." She was born, and lived and died in Michigan, her girlhood years being passed upon a farm near Marshall; began contributing to the public press at fourteen years of age; taught in the schools of Detroit, and at the age of twenty-seven married Dr. C. C. Lathrap, surgeon in the Ninth Michigan Cavalry. Removing to Jackson it was not long before her ability as a revivalist and preacher became known and she was licensed to preach by the Methodist church. At the first convention of the National W. C. T. U. in 1874 she was one of its leading spirits, but it was not until 1881 that she accepted the presidency for the state of Michigan. Mrs. Lathrap was a great sufferer for a year before her death, but dauntlessly bore with her "prison house of pain" until the inevitable was faced and smilingly greeted. Her home life was singularly harmonious, her husband being of great assistance to his wife in her marvelous work, while her relations to the aged mother who lived with her were always childlike, affectionate and reverential. "She made a record brilliant as a star and enduring as the granite of old Scotia, whence came her sturdy ancestry. She had the wit of that Irish race, a strain of whose blood was in her own ; she had the broad, bright outlook of the great West where

she was reared ; she had the generous, sisterly sympathy of the movement that swept her into its deep current and bore her on to fame
and death." Such is our Chieftain's tribute to Mary T. Lathrap.

MRS. JANE STAPLER.

A unique figure in our ranks was a veteran white-ribboner who
was "promoted" March 23, 1895. Mrs. Jane Stapler, of Tahlequah,
for many years president of the W. C. T. U. of Indian Territory, came
of a long line of Cherokee chiefs. She was born in Georgia, from which
state she was forced to emigrate with her parents and her tribe when a
little child, because white men had discovered gold upon the red man's
territory. Mrs. Stapler's first temperance work was in connection with
the "Sons and Daughters of Temperance," before the war, and when the
W. C. T. U. was organized in the Territory, she was chosen its standard
bearer. None of the delegates to the Atlanta convention in 1889 will
forget the meaningful words of this aged woman: "You don't know, my
sisters, what it means to me to come back after an interval of generations
to the state where I was born and be welcomed so tenderly by my comrades of the white ribbon who are fighting with me against the fire water
that has been the curse of my race as well as your own." Mrs. Stapler's
husband was a wealthy white merchant from the East and her sons are
leading merchants in Tahlequah. She was long the Lady Bountiful in
the territory and an intelligent, thoughtful Christian woman who has
dignified the whole Indian race.

ELLA F. M. WILLIAMS.

Little did we think when we requested for this book a biographical
sketch of the President of the Dominion of Canada and Treasurer of
the World's W. C. T. U. that it would find a place among the "Promoted." The sketch from which we glean the following facts was dic-
tated by Mrs. Williams herself not two days before her death, and when
received at Headquarters our faithful, loving comrade was at rest.

Mrs. Williams was of New England descent, her father, Rev. N. S.
Dickinson, being for more than thirty years a Congregational minister in
Massachusetts and well known before the civil war for his fearless advocacy of antislavery and prohibition principles. The greater part of
her early life was spent near Boston, where, for the most part, her education was personally conducted by her father. Later she attended

MARY T. LATHRAP.

Wheaton Seminary, graduating in 1869. After teaching two years she married Charles T. Williams, a business man of Cambridge. Removing to Montreal, Canada, in 1874, Mr. and Mrs. Williams entered with much enthusiasm into temperance and mission work, and when the first W. C. T. U. was organized in that town Mrs. Williams became its corresponding secretary. She served the Provincial Union as superintendent of Flower Mission work and recording secretary ; and the Dominion W. C. T. U. as superintendent of Flower Missions, as treasurer, and from 1892 until her lamented death, March 28, 1895, as president. In 1891 at the World's W. C. T. U. Convention in Boston she was elected treasurer of that organization.

A woman of marked individuality, one of Mrs. Williams' chief characteristics was her entire consecration. Her impulse was ever to give prominence to the work rather than to the worker, and in referring to her own connection with the white-ribbon movement she emphasizes the point not that she was a help to the W. C. T. U., but that "the work was a great help to her." So pronounced was her executive ability that positions of honor and trust were constantly urged upon her, and besides the onerous duties of a World's and National officer of the W. C. T. U. she found time for church and missionary interests, and had just resigned after four years service as treasurer of the Congregationalist Woman's Board of Canada.

So, one by one our leaders are gathering home, and as "we follow that way" our hopes naturally center upon the army of bright, consecrated young women who, as the gaps are made in our ranks, stand ready with earnest purpose and a courage tried and true to take their places at the front.

OTHER LEADERS.

Mrs. Caroline Brown Buell, for fourteen years corresponding secretary of the National W. C. T. U., may be counted both well-known and well loved among white-ribboners. The office came to her when very much of the W. C. T. U. work was new and untried, and to her it is indebted for the inception of many plans and the development of many more. Bereft of her husband when scarcely out of her teens by the cruel fortunes of our civil war, she devoted herself to her son, and when he no longer needed her she was ready to consecrate her powers of mind and heart to the greater war which should rid her country of the evil of intemperance. To this cause she brought a well-trained mind, a ready pen and a genius for execution. Mrs. Buell is a true New England, of *Mayflower* stock on the mother's side; on the father's she traces her ancestry to the Plantagenets and possesses true Yankee equipoise under all circumstances.

Miss Esther Pugh, well known to white-ribboners as former Treasurer of the National W. C. T. U., is one of the original Ohio crusaders, a Quaker by birth and training and a finely educated woman. She is a born journalist, inheriting a genius in this direction from her father, who for many years was proprietor and manager of the *Cincinnati Chronicle*. For four years she had charge of *Our Union*, two years as editor, two as publisher. She has made extensive trips through various states, lecturing and organizing, everywhere leaving the people more interested in our work than she found them, because more enlightened concerning it. After sixteen years of service, dating almost from the formation of the National Union, and nine years of which the treasurer's office was unsalaried, Miss Pugh resigned at the Chicago Convention in 1893, and retired from official life.

Mrs. Harriet B. Kells, was among the first of Southern women to take up W. C. T. U. work, and resigned a fine position as teacher for that purpose. As editor of the *Mississippi White Ribbon*, she made our principles felt throughout the entire South, and upon the death of Miss Julia Ames was called to the editorial force of the *Union Signal*. She ably filled

MRS. ELLA F. M. WILLIAMS.

MRS. ZERALDA G. WALLACE.

MRS. HARRIET B. KELLS.

that position for three years, when failing health made it necessary for her to seek a milder climate. Of Huguenot and Covenanter ancestry Mrs. Kells is richly endowed with the moral force which dares and the intellectual power which makes good that daring. She is a thinker with the world's best thought and a writer of great ability.

Mrs. Zerelda G. Wallace, known as the "Deborah" of the W. C. T. U., was born in Kentucky in 1817, and was for seven years president of the Indiana state union. She was the second wife of David Wallace, at the time of his marriage Lieutenant-Governor of Indiana, afterwards Governor of that state and Member of Congress. General Lew Wallace, the famous author of "Ben Hur," is his son, and our "Mother" Wallace is the original of that magnificent character, Ben Hur's mother. Mrs. Wallace has occupied from the first a leading place in the W. C. T. U. movement; was the first woman to offer a resolution in the National Convention condemning the use of wine at the communion table ; and presented the first resolution asking for woman's ballot on the temperance question. She has cradled three generations in her arms and earned a true title to the most devoted motherhood.

Mrs. Mary A. Livermore is a name which is not only national but international. Born, bred and educated in Boston, the wife of a Universalist minister of exceptionally fine abilities and character, his associate as editor of the church paper, the leader of the forces of women in the civil war when sanitary conferences and hospital administration engaged the attention of the public ; later one of the chosen leaders of the woman suffrage movement and a member of the editorial corps of the *Woman's Journal;* for many years president of the W. C. T. U. of Massachusetts, and still its honorary president ; a contributor to leading publications, and the author of a famous book, "My Recollections of the War," Mrs. Livermore has made a splendid record. For thirty years she has been conspicuous on the lecture platform, and has been heard in the lyceum courses of the country year after year in nearly every state of the Union, as well as in England and Scotland. Notwithstanding her many years of hard service, she is still in vigorous health, and has recently celebrated her fiftieth wedding anniversary with great éclat at her beautiful home in Melrose, Massachusetts.

Rev. Henrietta G. Moore is one of the great host which came out of that baptism, the crusade, to give their lives to the prohibition cause. Hers was not a total abstinence home; the wine cup had been the legacy of generations and she tasted the bitteruess which comes through the curse of strong drink. While still teaching she became secretary of the Ohio union, and did this work so well she was called to leave the school-room and enter the field as an organizer. In the midst of journeyings and incessant labors she found time to prepare for the ministry and after due examination was welcomed to an honored place in the Universalist church. Miss Moore has had repeated calls to settled pastoral work, but has not yet determined to turn aside from her itinerant labors in the Woman's Christian Temperance Union.

Mary A. Lathbury is a name which the W. C. T. U. is proud to place on the list of "Some of our women." As a child she was fond of picture-making and of illustrating her own poems. After leaving school she taught drawing and painting and in 1874, at the urgent request of Bishop Vincent, went to New York to engage in editorial work. She endeared herself to multitudes of children as the "Aunt Mary" who with her gifts and pen and pencil made the *Sunday School Advocate* a constant delight. She was also a contributor to *St. Nicholas* and *Wide Awake.* There is not a line she has penned or drawn which does not help to lead the human heart to a clearer appreciation of that sweet saying which must have been the motto of her long and high endeavor: "To be carnally minded is death ; but to be spiritually minded is life and peace." Of the many hymns Mary Lathbury has written, "Day is Dying in the West," and "Break Thou the Bread of Life" are perhaps the best known.

Mrs. Alice J. Harris is well known to the National Convention through her magnificent voice and abilities as musical director. She is the wife of Hon. Wm. G. Harris of Boston, has been for some years the soprano of Tremont Temple church and the chief musical attraction at the leading Chautauquas. Mrs. Harris is so generous a woman that her notes have never proved golden to the white-ribboners except as addressed to the ear. Her staunch total abstinence principles and frank avowal of the same have helped us not a little, and we regard her as the prima-donna of the W. C. T. U.

Mrs. Jennette G. Hauser, formerly President of the W. C. T. U. of India, was born in Illinois, educated in Wisconsin, and went as a bride to India. Returning after seven years to America she gave such time as could be spared from family cares to temperance work and the Woman's Foreign Missionary Society. She is the author of "The Orient and Its People," long a text-book for woman's missionary societies of all denominations ; also author of "Notes on the Light of Asia." Later she took up her residence in India for the second time and in 1893 the World's W. C. T. U. appointed her leader of their work there. New unions were formed, and the India union of scattered members organized. It now enrolls nearly three hundred. The monthly publication, *The White Ribbon,* was begun by Mrs. Hauser and turned over to her successor in office with an assured existence and a surplus in its treasury. Mrs. Hauser is now in America, where her costume lectures are in great demand.

Rev. Anna Howard Shaw, M. D., National Chairman of Overflow Meetings, was born in Newcastle-upon-Tyne, England. She removed to America with her parents when four years old, became a teacher in Michigan when only fifteen, received a local preacher's license from the Methodist church, graduated in Theology at the Boston University in 1878, and in Medicine in 1885. She was pastor of the Methodist church at Hingham, Massachusetts, and for seven years at East Dennis, Massachusetts ; also of the Congregational church at Dennis, Massachusetts ; was ordained in the Methodist Protestant church in 1880, and is still a member of the New York Conference of that denomination. She has now given up local parish work for the larger parish —the world. Audiences are conciliated by her cultured manner, enlivened by her wit, and captured by her logic. She is vice-president of the National American Woman Suffrage Association, and of the National Council of Women.

Mrs. Mary Lowe Dickinson, President of the National Council of Women of the United States, and a loyal white-ribboner, was born and educated in New England and became a teacher when very young. Her marriage to John B. Dickinson, a wealthy banker of New York City, changed her life to one of even wider opportunities for social and philanthropic work and she entered actively into many lines of charitable effort. Some time after the death of her husband came the loss of fort-

une, which threw her back again into the ranks of workingwomen.
The teacher's life was resumed, the pen which had been in time past
used little except for pleasure, became now the servant as well as the
substitute for the personal work and care that had been given to the
problems of the poor.   Her editorial work in many journals, her power
of character-drawing and the story-teller's gift, as well as the beautiful
poems, reveal wonderful facility of expression and variety of style.

Mrs. Dickinson is the General Secretary of the order of the King's
Daughters, and has been, since its birth, actively engaged in the charge
of its work all over the world.   She established its magazine, *The Silver
Cross*, of which she has been the only editor.   She was secretary of
the New York Bible Society, and president of the Woman's National
Indian Association ; was offered positions in seven of our leading institutions of learning ; was made Professor of Literature in the University of Denver, and at the close of her service there was made Emeritus
Professor, and given also a lectureship in English literature.   The chair
was endowed and given Mrs. Dickinson's name.   Warmly interested
in the cause of temperance she served for several years as the joint
editor of the *American Reformer*.   Mrs. Dickinson is a business woman
in every fiber and an indefatigable worker.   Something of the masterful way acquired by teachers is in her manner, only softened by a charming personality and a kindly nature that makes her a delightful person
to meet.

Mrs. Marion B. Baxter, prohibition orator and writer, is a direct
descendant of the Puritans and a woman of strong convictions.   Her
father was an Advent minister and her mother a gracious woman to
whose gentle companionship Mrs. Baxter says she owes all she is.   In
1875 she married C. E. K. Baxter and they have one daughter.   Mrs.
Baxter is a success in her chosen field of effort.   Of handsome and vigorous physique, with clear, deep and ringing voice, and a sparkling
humor, she presents her arguments in a style peculiarly her own.   She
has addressed audiences from Prince Edward Island to the Pacific.   A
radical Prohibitionist, she was for two years president of the White Rose
League of Michigan.   Her home is now Harvey, Illinois, and she is
superintendent of the Social Purity department of the Central Union of
Chicago.

Miss Elizabeth Upham Yates, one of our most attractive platform speakers, is a native of Maine, and a graduate of the Boston

School of Expression. She spent several years in China and has given a graphic description of oriental life in her book, "Glimpses into Chinese Homes." Greatly interested in the progress of women in all lands, Miss Yates, since her return to this country has served the W. C. T. U. as National lecturer of the Franchise department. She has spoken before the legislatures of various states in advocacy of woman's ballot and devotes most of her time to that phase of the work. She was appointed delegate from Maine to the World's W. C. T. U. Convention in London.

Mrs. Ada M. Bittenbender, of Lincoln, Nebraska, was four years attorney and five years superintendent of the Legislative department of the National. She has made several admirable arguments before Congressional committees in support of measures and petitions presented to Congress by the W. C. T. U. and it was under her superintendency that Congress enacted the law raising the age of protection to sixteen years. Mrs. Bittenbender is her husband's law partner and has been admitted to the Supreme Court of her own state and of the United States. She has published a valuable hand-book, "The National Prohibitory Amendment Guide," and is now engaged in bringing out a work entitled, "Uncle Sam's Drunkard Factories"; a story showing their unconstitutionality and procedures for abolishing them under existing laws. She is president of an incorporated company, one object of which is "to begin and prosecute test cases to obtain decisions of State and Federal Courts."

Madam Demorest is a white-ribboner with a business ability of a very high order. She is one of the Board of Directors of the Woman's Temperance Publishing Association, and was a W. C. T. U. Commissioner for the Columbian Exposition. She is one of the most active women in philanthropic and literary circles of New York City, and has been for years a prominent member of Sorosis, one of the most famous woman's clubs of that city. Since the death of her husband, one of prohibition's stalwart champions, Madam Demorest has devoted her attention to the carrying forward of the work inaugurated by him, and which has proved so helpful to the cause—the Demorest Medal Contests.

Mrs. Caroline E. Merrick, of New Orleans, is the daughter of one of Andrew Jackson's chief coadjutors in the army. Reared in the depths

of Louisiana, and never knowing anything but the portion of a slave-
holder's child, Mrs. Merrick always perceived the abominable character
of the institution, and when our boys in blue went South, and the bul-
lets rained and cannons roared but a short distance from her beautiful
plantation home, she had the soldiers, gray and blue alike, brought to
her house, and gave herself and all she had to caring for them. Mrs.
Merrick has an irresistible drollery in her composition, a humorous gift
that has carried her through the dark places of her life and gilded the
brightness of her happier years. She is so bright of pen that if she had
not been a rich woman she would have made her mark in literature. It
was her good fortune to meet one of New England's noblest young
men, Judge Edwin Merrick, a man of the finest culture and training,
who went South long before the war, and became Chief Justice of
Louisiana under the Confederacy. In their attractive home they have
been at the center of all that was most cultured and intellectual,
philanthropic and religious in New Orleans for a quarter of a century.

Mrs. Mary M. Love was for five years white-ribbon standard
bearer in Australia, returning to represent the work at the Boston Convention in 1891. Previous to that time she had been state evangelist in
Virginia; since then she has again taken up active work in her native
state, first as preacher in the Baptist church, where fifty years ago her
grandfather was pastor, then as co-pastor of a church in Parkersburg,
West Virginia, which position she resigned to devote her whole time to
W. C. T. U. work. She is an earnest Bible student and has an unwavering faith in the success of the W. C. T. U. in all its lines of work.

Mrs. Mary Seymour Howell, one of the lecturers for the Franchise department, was a leader in the crusade in New York, her native
state, and early became imbued with the idea that the ballot for woman
was the solution of the temperance question. She was appointed by
Mrs. Elizabeth Cady Stanton to represent the National American
Woman Suffrage Association at the National Council of Women at Washington, D. C., in 1891. Mrs. Howell has a classical education ; has been
a teacher, a conductor of teachers' institutes, and has spoken for the
advancement of woman before Congress and many State Legislatures.

Mrs. Mary B. Jones of Philadelphia is one of the most acute
minds in the white-ribbon army. She is the wife of Joshua R. Jones,

known throughout the world for his specialty of Bible publishing. Mrs. Jones is a graduate of the Girls' High School of Philadelphia, and has been prominent in W. C. T. U. work for eighteen years ; was state president three years, vice-president ten years, and is now president of the Philadelphia union, which numbers nearly four hundred members and which through her tremendous energy and business ability has recently acquired ownership of large and handsome headquarters.

Mrs. Lizzie D. Carhart modestly refers to herself as "a quiet woman who has chiefly worked in quiet places." Reared and educated in the most conservative manner, she says that whatever she has been privileged to do in a public way is the result of helping words from other workers, notably Miss Willard, who awakened the first thought of a possibility of endeavor beyond the little circle of local work. She has been treasurer of the W. C. T. U. of Iowa since its organization and is well known to the National organization as president of Iowa W. C. T. U. during the constitutional amendment campaign of 1881–83.

Mrs. Maria B. Gordon, for fifteen years president of the Boston W. C. T. U., is a woman of indomitable purpose along the lines of Christian effort to which she has especially devoted herself—temperance and missionary work. She is the wife of the late Rev. Dr. A. J. Gordon, our temperance "Hercules," one of Boston's leading divines, who nobly supported her in all her undertakings. Mrs. Gordon is a born leader and plans a campaign for no-license or prohibitory amendment with the skill of a general. She is a most acceptable public speaker, her voice uttering no uncertain sound on the vexed questions of the nation.

Mrs. Helen Dickinson Harford is a graduate of the State Normal College, Albany, New York. In 1887 she left the position of teacher to enter the field for the W. C. T. U. She removed from Kansas City, Missouri, to Oregon in 1891 and at the following state convention was elected recording secretary of Oregon. In 1894 she received the nomination for state superintendent of public instruction, polling a larger vote than any other candidate on the ticket. For two years she has been a National lecturer of the Franchise department.

Mrs. Linda T. Rhoades of Allegheny, Pennsylvania, is a prominent Y leader. In 1857 she went with her husband to New York, where, in the Asylum for Destitute Children, she first realized the curse of the drink traffic. She joined the W. C. T. U. ranks just after the crusade, devoting herself chiefly to the young woman's branch. She still has a Home for Destitute Children where are received the children of intemperate parents. Mrs. Rhoades was delegate from Pennsylvania to the World's Convention in London.

Mrs. Sarah M. Perkins of Cleveland, Ohio, is a Universalist minister. At eighteen she was a teacher, afterwards attended school at the old Academy in Adams, Massachusetts, and at twenty-three married Rev. Orrin Perkins, a talented clergyman. She was an early abolitionist, an early Prohibitionist, is the author of many Sunday-school books, has lectured upon temperance and woman suffrage in nearly every state in the Union, and organized the Indian Territory for the W. C. T. U. Mrs. Perkins is of a most cheery nature, witty as well as wise. She is the editor of the *True Republic,* a monthly paper which has a large circulation.

Mrs. Esther Taylor Housh, became known to white-ribboners as editor of *The Woman at Work*, a bright and helpful magazine, published in Louisville, Kentucky. Later on Mrs. Housh and her capable son Frank established their magazine in Brattleboro, Vermont, and Mrs. Housh became president of Vermont W. C. T. U., being still its honorary president. She is the daughter of a pioneer minister of Ohio, an old-time abolitionist, and was carefully educated and trained in home-keeping; was National superintendent of Press work for five years, and is now corresponding secretary of Massachusetts W. C. T. U. and editor of its state paper, *Our Message.*

Mrs. Eugenia F. St. John, who, with her husband, has been among our most successful evangelists, is a self-educated woman. She began teaching at fourteen, later on took an academical and normal course, and taught in the public schools eleven years. She has been seven times elected as a delegate to the National Convention, and is a member of the National Prohibition Committee. Mrs. St. John was in 1889 ordained as minister in the Methodist Protestant church, and was the first woman in the United States to sit in the General Conference. She is just closing a two years successful pastorate in Kansas City, Kansas.

Mrs. Wilbur F. Crafts began public service as a school teacher in Davenport, Iowa, at fifteen, and was soon after promoted to teacher of primary methods in the Winona Normal school. Being invited to present her methods to the Sabbath-school teachers of Minnesota in state convention assembled, she was at once called by D. L. Moody to do the same for a whole series of conventions. Her work for temperance has been chiefly in four ways: (1) In promoting, with her husband, the introduction, continuance and use of the quarterly temperance lessons; (2) in the preparation, with Mrs. Mary B. Willard, of the first series of the Loyal Legion Quarterly lessons; (3) in contributing a long series of blackboard temperance lessons for *The Temperance Banner;* (4) in blackboard temperance addresses to children and teachers at Sabbath-school conventions. Both Mr. and Mrs. Crafts are counted by the W. C. T. U. as among its strongest helpers both by reason of their official relation to Sunday-school work and their personal relation to and interest in white-ribbon effort.

Mrs. Lavinia B. Benedict, of Iowa, better known as "Mother" Benedict, was born in the woods of Ohio in 1823, and at thirty-three became a recognized minister in the Quaker church. Widowed at fifty-five, she has since devoted her life to rescuing and providing for unfortunate girls. As the result of her efforts two Homes are in operation in Iowa —one in Des Moines, one in Decorah. Mrs. Benedict, now in her seventy-second year, personally superintends the Decorah Home, and has written a book, "Woman's Work for Woman" giving an account of her labors.

Mrs. Sarah D. La Fetra, of Washington, District of Columbia, has been a powerful factor in bringing victory for our society at the very headquarters of rum and politics. Her achievements could never have been possible to any woman of less kindly nature or less indefatigable activity. The "Shelter for Women," the gospel temperance meetings, the great popular mass-meetings, the well-conducted press work, the thorough canvass by petition, the hearings arranged at the Capitol, the large-hearted liberality in bringing speakers from a distance and entertaining them at her own expense in the beautiful temperance Hotel Fredonia, presided over by Dr. and Mrs. La Fetra,—all evince the adaptedness of this devoted pair to help on our white-ribbon work at the nation's capital.

Alice Stone Blackwell says that the most noteworthy fact in her life is that she is her mother's daughter. When Alice was a baby Lucy Stone let her furniture be sold for taxes and wrote to the assessors a protest against taxation without representation with her baby on her knee. Alice was born at Orange, New Jersey, in 1857; graduated at Boston University in 1881; began work as one of the staff of the *Woman's Journal* in the same year and has for many years been one of its editors. She is recording secretary of the National American Woman Suffrage Association and associate National superintendent of Franchise in the W. C. T. U.

Mrs. Amelia E. Sanford, of Bloomington, Illinois, is of New England birth. Widowed when quite young she was enrolled for nine years among the teachers of the Bloomington High School, succeeded Mrs. Carhart as Dean of the Woman's College in the Northwestern University at Evanston, and held the Latin professorship in Adrian College, Michigan. With such equipment for service and with unflinching devotion to every good cause, she is a worthy leader in the W. C. T. U. forces of Illinois. Mrs. Sanford is state W. C. T. U. treasurer, editor of the *Illinois Watch-Tower*, and was one of the Prohibition party nominees in 1894 for University Trustee.

Mrs. Ella Eaton Kellogg, is the wife of Dr. J. H. Kellogg, proprietor of the great Sanitarium at Battle Creek, Michigan. She was educated at Alfred University, and at the age of nineteen received the degree of A. L., and later that of A. M. Mrs. Kellogg was for some years National superintendent of the department of Hygiene and in 1885 became associate superintendent of the Purity department, her special charge being Mothers' Meetings. Both Dr. and Mrs. Kellogg are devoted temperance workers and give talent, time and money to the upbuilding of the work. Having no children of their own they have gathered about them in their home a number of orphan children to whom they give the watchful tender care of "own" parents.

Mrs. Mary E. Cheney, of Boston, has been aptly designated by Miss Willard as "one of our gentlest and bravest white-ribboners." She entered into the work of the W. C. T. U. with all the fervor of her nature, and there are few departments of the organization which have not shared her sympathy and co-operation. Mrs. Cheney has been state superintendent for our National organ, *The Union Signal*, and for the state paper, *Our Message*, for many years, and has done valiant service for the cause along these lines.

Mrs. Anna M. Bain is the wife of George W. Bain, the noted temperance orator. When Miss Willard organized the W. C. T. U. in Kentucky she led Anna Bain out of her quiet home-life into the presidency of a local union. She soon after became state president, which place she held until her health demanded retirement. As president of the Home of Mercy in Lexington she is doing a great work in rescuing fallen women. She is president of the missionary society of the M. E. Church South, and active in other church and charity work. Mrs. Bain possesses an exceptionally sweet and modest nature which controls without dictating, and she wins her way over difficulties by the resistless force of love.

Mrs. Sara Bull of Cambridge, Massachusetts, at one time National superintendent of the department of Sanitary and Economic Cookery, is one of the leading women of that great literary center. She is the daughter of Mrs. A. C. Thorpe, before her lamented death one of the central figures in the W. C. T. U. of the old Bay State, and widow of Ole Bull, the noted violinist. For years their home was the celebrated "Elmwood" of James Russell Lowell, and later, a stately mansion near "Craigie House," the home of Longfellow, one of whose daughters is the wife of Mrs. Bull's only brother.

Mrs. L. D. Plumb of Wheaton, Illinois, is a graduate of Oberlin College, and entered the W. C. T. U. ranks eighteen years ago. She was a charter member of the Woman's Temperance Publishing Association and of the National Temperance Hospital board, to both of which she still belongs. Mrs. Plumb is *par excellence* a woman of business. She is vice-president of the bank in Streator, Illinois, and president of the Mortgage and Loan Company of Iowa. Her husband was a brother beloved of all white-ribboners. He it was, who, in the dark-

est hour of the W. T. P. A.'s history, tided it over with kindliest
words of encouragement and financial help. His wife was his help-
meet in all his business affairs, and when they dropped from his lifeless
hand she took up bravely, for her children's sake, the double burden
of sorrow and responsibility.

Mrs. Elizabeth G. Hibben, one of Illinois' prominent workers,
was one of the founders of *The Signal*, the Illinois paper which was afterward incorporated as *The Union Signal*, and followed Miss Willard as
state president when the latter was elected to the National. She was
left a widow at twenty-one with an only son, now Rev. John Grier Hibben, professor of Logic in Princeton College. Mrs. Hibben has filled
many offices in the W. C. T. U., local, district, state and National, in all
of which she is efficient and beloved.

Mrs. Lucie B. Tyng, of Peoria, Illinois, is a very queen among
women, possessing rare executive ability, joined to such sweet womanliness as makes her home ideal, her presence and influence always sought,
always a benediction. That she is not a woman of one idea is evidenced
by the fact that she is president of the Woman's Christian Association,
the Memorial Day Association, and the Hospital Board ; is actively identified with all charitable and church work of Peoria, and has just been
elected, by a most gratifying majority, upon the school board, the only
woman holding this position of trust and honor in that city. Mrs.
Tyng—her face always "like the morning"—has for several years been
prominently before the National Convention as chairman of the committee upon telegrams, her efficiency being here, as everywhere, clearly
manifest.

Mrs. Rebecca Catherine Shuman, is a name that will always
be indissolubly linked with the Polyglot Petition. For four years a
large proportion of her time and thought was devoted to the prodigious
task of mounting fives miles of names on the rolls of muslin which were
to travel round the world. A diploma of honorable mention was presented to Mrs. Shuman by the World's Fair Board of Lady Managers
for the Petition as there exhibited. Mrs. Shuman's childhood's home
was in Pennsylvania. Her father, John Fertig, was an earnest worker
for the abolition of slavery and earned the name of "Father Mathew"

by his war upon liquor and tobacco. Her home is now in Evanston, Illinois, where she is the center of a charming family circle.

Miss Alice Briggs, was for nine years Miss Willard's Office Secretary and for six years Office Secretary of the World's W. C. T. U. She was a teacher in Illinois; became president of a district union; was National Press superintendent; then Press superintendent of the World's Union. She is faithfulness and capability incarnate and knows the W. C. T. U. and its great petition work as she does her own history.

Miss Irene Fockler, for five years one of Miss Willard's busy secretaries, two years associate superintendent of the Press department, World's and National W. C. T. U. and one year Office Secretary of National W. C. T. U., was born near Janesville, Wisconsin, of intelligent, progressive parents; attended the public schools during childhood and took elective studies in the Northwestern University, Evanston, Illinois, in 1879 and 1880. She has done reportorial work for leading newspapers in Chicago and New York, and has published both prose and verse in Chicago, Cincinnati, Washington, and Boston periodicals. She has been one of the corps of literary helpers at Rest Cottage, her specialty having been the sending out of literature and preparation of items for the press.

Mrs. Sarah J. Early, of Nashville, Tennessee, is an educated, successful and earnest leader among the colored women. She has been in the white-ribbon work for many years, is an eloquent and dignified platform speaker and possesses the respect and confidence of the white people of the South as well as that of her own race.

Many are the names which the editor would like to add to these pages, but if space were given to all W. C. T. U. women who deserve honorable mention, this book would grow to such proportions that nobody would buy it. The white-ribbon movement is so steadily widening and new workers are so constantly coming to the front that it is impossible within the prescribed limits of a sketch-book to give more than a small part of our roll of honor. We realize that the thousands of women in the rank and file of the white-ribbon army are the elements which constitute the real strength and power of our organization ; that it is their loyalty and consecration which makes possible the act ve-ments of our leaders ; and that to the quiet workers of our local Unions who each in her own little corner looks faithfully and well to the "little" things, belongs whatever of praise and of virtue attaches to the W. C. T. U. as the result of its magnificent record for God and humanity.

www.ingramcontent.com/pod-product-compliance
Lightning Source LLC
Chambersburg PA
CBHW032008060726
47497CB00017B/2394